Samantha Hunter lives in Syracuse, New York, where she writes full-time for Harlequin. When she's not plotting her next story, Sam likes to work in her garden, quilt, cook, read and spend time with her husband and their dogs. Most days you can find Sam chatting on the Harlequin Blaze boards at Harlequin.com, or you can check out what's new, enter contests or drop her a note at her website, samanthahunter.com.

Meg Maguire worked as a record store snob, a lousy barista, a decent designer and an overenthusiastic penguin handler, before becoming a writer. She loves crafting no-nonsense, working-class heroes with capable hands and lousy grammar. She was a 2010 Golden Heart finalist, and a two-time RT Reviewers' Choice Award nominee. Meg writes full-time and lives in the Pacific Northwest with her own bearded hero.

Debbi Rawlins grew up in rural Hawaii but has always loved Western movies and books. If she remembers correctly, her first crush was on a cowboy. He was an actor in the role of a cowboy, but then she was only eleven. Years later she attended her first rodeo on the island of Maui. The next was in Houston, Texas, where she first started writing for Harlequin. Now, more than fifty-five books later, she lives on a few acres in gorgeous rural Utah, surrounded by four dogs, five cats and a trio of goats.

Samantha Hunter
Meg Maguire
Debbi Rawlins

Wild Holiday Nights

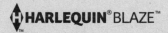

HARLEQUIN® BLAZE™

ISBN-13: 978-0-373-79829-2

Wild Holiday Nights

Copyright © 2014 by Harlequin Books S.A.

The publisher acknowledges the copyright holders of the
individual works as follows:

Holiday Rush
Copyright © 2014 by Samantha Hunter

Playing Games
Copyright © 2014 by Meg Maguire

All Night Long
Copyright © 2014 by Debbi Rawlins

Recycling programs
for this product may
not exist in your area.

Printed in U.S.A.

CONTENTS

HOLIDAY RUSH

Samantha Hunter

Happy Holidays to all my wonderful readers, whether you are home or elsewhere. Enjoy!

1

CALLA MICHAELS NEVER wanted to see another holly leaf or berry ever again. She'd always loved the dark green holiday plant, with its pointy leaves and ripe, red berries. But after hand-shaping two hundred of them from gum paste—accented with twenty-four-karat gold leaf—for the holiday wedding cake she was decorating, she was over it.

Still, while she was tired of Christmas themes, she was doing the work she loved. Good thing, since she had one more wedding cake to make before she was done. Spring and summer would bring much more variety, she mused as she applied the last berry to the delicate edge of the pristine white cake before standing back to assess her work.

Perfect. Absolutely gorgeous. The decoration wasn't the only thing that was custom—the inside of the cake had to be as special as the outside, and Calla often created flavor profiles requested by clients. This one was a butter-mint cake with white chocolate filling between the layers. The next cake would be rum-pecan.

All she had to do was load this one into the truck and get it to the restaurant downtown. They would store it for the wedding the day after next. Then she could take a short break before she started work on the final cake, which was needed for Christmas Day—only ten days away.

It didn't escape her that she still had a ton of shopping to do. If she couldn't be home for Christmas this year, the least she could do was to send some gifts from the Big Apple. It didn't make up for her not being there, especially not for her mother, but Calla really had no choice.

She had to work straight through Christmas Eve, then she would take Christmas Day off, sleep and get back to it the next day. She'd managed to contract for three New Year's cakes, which was a lot to do in one week, so she had to keep moving. Those orders would give her enough to pay the rent and supplies through January.

Her funky little storefront in Chelsea had been expensive, but it was a good location. One she could barely afford, but the eclectic local food scene helped her visibility. Still, she'd have to double her business in the coming year to stay alive, and she really needed to hire part-time help.

That meant there was no way she could go home for Christmas. It was difficult getting her family to understand. Hers was a law enforcement clan—even her mother worked at the sheriff's office. Her father and brothers all worked for assorted law enforcement agencies. Her sister was a firefighter.

Calla baked cakes for a living.

She could still hear her mother's voice on the phone. *Calla, I understand when your brothers or sister have to work a shift over the holidays, but how is it that you can't ever seem to make it home?*

Her siblings saved lives, after all. Her mother hadn't said that explicitly, but she might as well have. Calla knew her career choice puzzled them. They had no idea how competitive the big-city food scene was. But this was her dream, and it had taken everything she had to get here. It was going to take even more to stay.

Calla's Cakes was the result of arduous training at culinary school and graduating at the top of her class. That had been followed by internships at some of the best bakeries. Now she was trying to make it on her own in the middle of one of the biggest cities in the world. Not an endeavor for the faint-hearted. Unfortunately, it had meant missing several holidays along the way, but that was the cost of running her business.

Her mother had suggested she come back to Houston and open a shop there, or in the small town near their ranch. That might have been a possibility if she had smaller goals, but

New York was where Calla had always wanted to be. She missed her family, but this city felt like home.

Being here pushed her to be at the top of her game—better than the best.

She loved her family, and they said they were proud of her, but as she'd pursued her ambitions, the gap had widened. They just didn't understand how she could be so passionate about her work.

What she did was important to the people she baked for, though, and it was why they were willing to pay her a premium for something special. Something unique that would become one of their most cherished memories. It wasn't life or death, but it was part of her customers' dreams. Their happily ever afters.

She smiled as she rolled the cart holding the cake to the back room. She'd load it into a refrigerated case for safe transport, and then she'd get a night's sleep. She could do some shopping tomorrow, pack gifts off in the mail, before starting the next cake.

Opening the back doors, she patted her pockets and realized she didn't have the keys to the van.

She went back in and found them on the counter, then returned to load up the cake. As she started to do that, though, the hairs on her neck stood up. She wasn't alone.

"Stay quiet and you won't get hurt. Just show me the cash drawer now."

Equal parts fear and fury had Calla shaking from head to toe, and her voice shook, too, as she spoke.

"Does this look like a doughnut shop? I don't have a cash drawer. My customers pay by credit card, and there's no cash kept on the premises. Not even a register, which you would have seen if you'd looked through the window first."

Something sharp jutted into her spine as hard fingers grabbed her shoulder.

"I don't believe you. A fancy place like this has to have some money around somewhere."

Tears stung as she wondered, for a brief second, if she would ever go home for Christmas again. If she had listened to her mother and closed for the holiday, maybe she wouldn't be in this spot now.

"I have some money in my purse. And my credit cards, too. That's all," she said as calmly as she could, hoping to placate her attacker—and hoping that money was all he was really after. He was welcome to it. There wasn't much, and her cards were almost maxed out buying everything she needed for the shop.

Suddenly, she wished she had taken more to the weapons and self-defense training her father and brothers had always tried to push on her.

"Where?"

"My purse is in my office. Go back through those doors and—"

"I think you and me will go back there and get it together," he said, his voice slurring a little. As if he'd been drinking or something.

Then Calla heard a noise in the alley behind the store, a door slamming and voices. Someone was out there, maybe someone from one of the neighboring businesses or apartments.

No way could she walk back into the dark recess of her office with this guy. There no one could see them. She'd be helpless.

"Help!" she yelled as loud as she could, tripping as she pulled sharply away, falling forward and scrambling across the floor toward the back door. "Help! I'm being robbed!"

Please, let someone hear me, she thought desperately as her attacker cursed and came forward after her. She spun around to see where he was. He was tall, young—maybe in his mid-twenties, she guessed, seeing his face as he rushed toward her.

No gun, she also noted with relief—until she saw the gleaming knife in his hands. She was close to the door, and the only thing between her and the intruder was the cake.

She scurried behind the cart and pushed hard, rolling the metal cart toward the thief. The dangerous-looking blade he'd been carrying slid across the floor as the cart—and her gorgeous cake—slammed into him.

"Hey, what's going on in there?" someone called from outside. Jack Samosa, the dry cleaner from two doors down, stepped inside, shocked as he took in the scene before him.

Before Calla could warn Mr. Samosa, who was an older man, he was almost knocked over as the robber ran out the door into the alley.

"What the... Calla, are you all right?" he asked as he rushed to her and helped Calla pick herself up from the floor.

She was still shaking as she nodded, unable to speak yet. Then she took in the scene before her.

The cake she'd just spent four days working on was now decorating her back-room floor. She stared at the mess, not answering Mr. Samosa though she heard him, in the distance, calling the police.

"Merry Christmas to me," she whispered, sliding back down to the floor to sit among the mess until the police arrived.

FOUR DAYS BEFORE CHRISTMAS, Gideon Stone walked along the streets of Chelsea, scanning the Christmas decorations and crowds as he searched for the storefront of Calla's Cakes. It had to be here somewhere. Finally he spotted the small silver sign with black script hanging high above the entry a few yards in front of him. People were gathered in front, watching something.

As soon as he joined them, he realized what they were watching: Calla.

It had been a few years since he'd seen her, but she was even lovelier than he remembered. Her dark brown hair was longer now, though pulled back in a severe braid at the moment. That only emphasized her ivory skin even more so— not tanned like it used to be in Texas—and huge green eyes.

The bakery window wasn't like anything he'd ever seen before, either. There weren't glass cases with rows of goodies, but a single, bright room with ovens, refrigerators at the back and worktables poised in front of the large windows where Calla apparently worked in front of an audience.

Then he remembered Nathan, her older brother and Gideon's friend, mentioning that. She called it performance baking—it was some new thing in the city. He hadn't had any idea what it meant at the time.

Calla seemed completely unaware of her onlookers as she sat sculpting a row of different-size bells from golden blocks of cake. As she finished one perfect bell, she looked up, showing it off to the group as they expressed their admiration. Calla smiled back and held up her finger in a gesture to wait. She gathered the scraps of cake from her carving and put them in small white cups, topping them with a dollop of something white and creamy before carrying them outside to her company.

The crowd cheered lightly as she emerged from the wrought iron door at the entrance and started passing out the cups of cake. Murmurs of appreciation rose from those gathered. Gideon waited until she handed a cup to him. He took it and didn't let go for a second as he waited for her to look up.

When she did, her lovely lips parted slightly and her eyes widened in surprise.

"Gideon? What are you doing here?"

She smiled, and he started to speak, but stopped when her smile faded.

"Nathan sent you, didn't he?"

She pulled away her hand before he could confirm or deny, though she'd hit the nail on the head the first time. He hadn't planned on lying about it, but he'd hoped she would be more receptive. Her family was simply worried, and he was doing them a favor.

At least he got some of the cake, topped with a fragrant whipped cream. As he put the small chunk to his lips, the aroma hit him first, the wafting scent of rum and nuts. Then the light, buttery texture floated over his tongue and took over his senses. It was the only time a piece of cake ever made him close his eyes in pleasure.

"Wow," he managed, wanting to enjoy it for as long as possible.

"Glad you like it."

He opened his eyes again to find Calla's cat-green gaze on him, her tone as chilly as the weather.

He almost said "wow" a second time, but swallowed it down with the last of the cake.

"You should have been here for the chocolate mocha she made the other day," a guy next to him said with a sigh of appreciation.

He'd met Calla once when Nathan had invited him over to their family ranch. That was eight years ago. She'd just graduated culinary school and had been home for a month over the summer, only twenty-two. Very pretty and very kissable.

Gideon had discovered that fact at a barbecue at the family ranch after they'd both had a little too much to drink. Though she had given him the green light for more than a kiss, he'd backed off. She was young, and she was his friend's sister. Moreover, she was his training officer's sister.

Definitely off-limits.

His eyes fell to her mouth. That hadn't changed at all.

"That might be the best thing I've ever put in my mouth," he said and watched color rise in the perfectly smooth, porcelain skin of her cheeks. His heart beat a little faster, and he had to get hold of his response.

She was *still* Nathan's sister. He had to remember that, though he wanted to take back his comment that the cake was the best thing he'd ever tasted.

"I suppose it's no coincidence that you're here? That you aren't on a Christmas vacation and happened by?"

He shook his head. She glared.

The people around them watched with increased interest.

"You can tell Nathan I'm fine and go back to Texas. There was no reason to come all this way," she said as she turned and walked into her bakery. She sat at the front table, going back to work as if he didn't even exist.

Gideon had been dismissed, and he paused for a beat out on the sidewalk.

"Well, are you just going to stand there? Go on in there after her," said the man who liked the chocolate cake. He winked at Gideon, nudging him with his elbow, obviously misinterpreting the whole thing.

But the guy was right. Gideon couldn't just walk away and leave it at that. He went inside, too, and closed the door behind him, aware they still had an audience.

"Calla. Can we talk? Maybe have lunch? My treat."

"It's past lunch, and I have work to do. I'm running behind."

She picked up a long spatula, fumbled it, dropped it to the floor with a clatter and cursed.

"He only wanted to make sure you were okay," Gideon offered.

"I'm fine. I don't have time for this nonsense right now."

"It's nonsense that Nathan was concerned about you being attacked and robbed? Especially when he had to find out about it through the police sheets? You never even called home."

Calla glared. "I spoke with my mother just a week or so ago."

"But you never told her what happened."

"Why? To worry them for no reason? I'm fine. And Nathan should keep his nose out of my business. You, too." She pointed the spatula at him with a few sharp jabs that punctuated her words. "I can take care of myself, in spite of what my family thinks. For goodness' sake, I'm an adult. I don't need my brothers sending their friends to check up on me." Over the top of the spatula she leveled him a look. "You did your duty. Go home."

With that, she went to the large sink in the corner of the room and turned on the hot water, scrubbing the spatula and then drying her hands, putting on new gloves.

When she stretched to reach something on an upper shelf, Gideon was distracted by how the chef's coat lifted and hinted at her curves underneath. Eight years had turned Calla from a girl into a woman, and he wasn't immune to that fact.

"Have they caught him?"

"I have no idea."

She went to her table and started working on more bells, ignoring him completely.

Gideon stood there and watched. Part of him felt ridiculous, because she was right. She was a thirty-year-old woman with her own business, who had lived in this city almost as long as she'd lived back in Texas. He could see that she was fine. Better than fine.

But he'd promised Nathan, and he didn't take that promise lightly. Gideon owed Nathan, big-time.

She stopped working again, smiling at the people outside as she winked and closed the window. Then she turned on him.

"Gideon, you're distracting me, and I can't afford—literally— to be distracted right now. You can tell Nathan I'm fine, I carry pepper spray and I'm as careful as I can be. I have a business to run, and people counting on me. I'm behind schedule after having to redo the cake that was destroyed the other night—which took two twenty-four-hour days to finish, by the way. I barely made it. Now I'm behind on this one, too, and you're not helping."

Gideon backed off a little, seeing the strain and the exhaustion that he hadn't caught before. She was stressed, probably afraid, but like the other members of the Michaels clan, she wasn't one to back down.

"When is this one supposed to be done?"

"Three days. I need to deliver it Christmas Eve, for a Christmas Day wedding, and it's not going as well as I'd hoped. I guess I'm distracted, but I keep messing up the carvings, and the first batch of batter didn't come out right."

"There was nothing wrong with that sample you just handed out, believe me."

"This one was good. I need to do it three more times now. I need forty-eight bells, and then I need to bake the base they will rest on. Then decorate."

Gideon looked at the bells on the counter. There were eight.

"It took me the last six hours to do these."

"You need to spend thirty more hours at this?"

"I should be able to make it, but it will be close, assuming no more goofs. Or distractions." She looked at him pointedly.

Gideon considered for a moment and stepped forward. "Maybe I could help."

Her eyebrows lifted, and she coughed out a laugh. "Are you hiding a culinary degree up your sleeve?"

"I do a lot of wood carving. How different can it be?"

Her lips fell apart, her expression shocked. "Are you kidding?"

"No. I mean, why not? If I can help you carve bells, that will speed things up for you, right? You can bake more cake while I do the carving. Consider it my apology for bugging you."

"These have to be done just so. It's cake, not wood."

"Let me try one. You might be surprised."

"No. You're just trying to find a way to stick around watching over me."

"Is that so bad?"

"Is this because we kissed once? Do you think you have some kind of special influence over me or something?"

"Do I?"

She crossed her arms over her front. "It was a long time ago, and it was only one kiss. I've kissed a lot of other guys since then."

Gideon wasn't sure he liked that idea, but shrugged.

"Fine. I'll make you a deal. Let me try one bell, and if I botch it, I go home, tell your family you're fine and leave you be. If I do okay, I'll stick around and help. At least for today."

"They can't be *okay,* they have to be *perfect.*"

"Okay. Then if I do *perfect,* I can stick around."

"Why are you pushing this? Why not just go?"

She sounded exasperated, but he knew he had her on the ropes.

"Because I owe Nathan. He saved my hide a few months ago, and frankly, I wouldn't even be standing here if it weren't for him. He asked me to do a simple favor for him, and I agreed. I'd like to keep my promise, even though it's clear that you're okay."

She stared at him for several long moments, her shoulders dropping as she pushed a block of cake across the table, relenting.

"Fine. It's a deal. You suck, you leave. Wash your hands, put on some gloves and let's see what you can do."

2

CALLA WATCHED GIDEON study the block of cake as if wondering where to start. He looked at her drawing, her cake plans, and then at the bells she'd done already. He didn't say a word.

Ever since she'd met him on the sidewalk, her heart hadn't settled down for a second. He had beautiful hands. Rough from the carpentry work that he did off hours, but nicely shaped. Masculine. They seemed too large for the delicate block of cake, but he was gentle, too.

The thought sent a shiver down her spine.

She hadn't thought she'd ever see him again. They'd shared a kiss eight years ago. She'd still been a virgin then, and she'd wanted more, but he'd backed off.

She'd only met one guy she liked in culinary school—Max—and she'd thought he'd be the one, but he had run as fast as he could in the opposite direction when he'd found out about her untouched status. He'd said he couldn't take that responsibility.

She'd been home for a month that summer with one goal on her mind—to change that status before she went back to the city. Gideon had appeared to be an excellent solution to her situation. They'd had sparks from the moment they'd met, and she'd *wanted* him. That had been new to her, too.

She'd walked with him across the field down by the old barns under the auspices of showing him around the ranch. She'd assumed they were on the same page—that he wanted the same thing she did. She'd known he was attracted to her. She'd been experienced enough to know *that*—and to try to take advantage of it.

When he'd kissed her, she'd known she'd made the right choice. His lips had melted her like candle wax at the first touch. His hands on her back, where he'd dragged his fingers back and forth along the skin under the band of her jeans, had set her on fire for the first time ever.

How could she ever forget those hands?

He could've had her right there and then, and oh, she had wanted him to do just that. But he'd stopped, made some vague excuse about it not being the right time or place and kissed her once more, lightly, before he'd walked back to the party. Alone.

Twice rejected, still a virgin. What Gideon had done was even worse than what Max had done. She'd been willing, warmed up and ready. She'd wanted him. She'd *chosen* him. It had been her first real attempt at seduction.

And he'd walked away.

It had taken awhile for the bruise on her ego to heal, and eventually she'd even had to give Gideon credit for doing the right thing. Kind of.

He'd been a few years older, wiser, and he was her brother's friend. His reasons were better than Max's, or at least nobler. Still, at the time it had hurt, and she didn't forget that either.

Now here he was, sitting in her bakery, holding cake in his hands as if it was a slab of wood, peeling off some delicate edges, thinly sliced, as he eased his way into the block.

She went to her drawer, grabbed another knife and some cake from the freezer and started another bell. She really didn't have any time to waste, since now she'd have to fix or redo whatever mess Gideon made. But if this little deal sent him on his way, it was worth it. He was far too distracting.

She started carving, silently inventing ways to kill her brother Nathan the next time she saw him. She was going to give her older brother an earful for dragging her into whatever was between the two men.

"There. How's that so far?"

Calla had been so lost in her ruminations that she wasn't paying attention to the minutes ticking by. Gideon's question shook her out of her trance to find him holding half of a perfectly shaped bell in his hand. He'd managed to get that far in the same time that she had barely made a dent.

"It's…great."

It was better than great. It was easily as good as hers.

"Don't sound so glum about it."

"I guess I should have studied carpentry instead of pastry," she muttered, knowing she was being a bad sport.

His bell might actually be better than hers, with a few little flourishes that she approved of. There was even a small smattering of applause outside the window as onlookers approved of his effort. She'd reopened the window not to embarrass him on purpose, but because she did so on a schedule, when the most people were walking by at intervals during the day.

A few more than usual were here this afternoon. Drawn in by her new helper? A number of them were female.

"So I get to stay and help you out?"

She frowned. "Looks like."

Then he put his cake and knife down and reached across the table to put his hand over hers.

Ay caramba.

Calla was pretty sure her entire body sizzled at the touch. Just like it had years ago.

She drew her hand away, self-conscious with people watching.

"Calla, listen, if you really want me to leave, I will. Would you mind, though, if I stop by the station and check in on their progress finding your attacker? And maybe let me take you to dinner tonight? I can't go back until tomorrow anyway."

Damn, he was being so nice. Calla knew she was being unreasonable.

"I'm sorry, I just… It's family stuff. I'm mad at Nathan, and at life, but I shouldn't take it out on you."

"Want to tell me about it?" he asked gently.

Calla let out a breath she was holding. He was being so

nice. She ended up telling him about the financial trouble the shop was in, her guilt about not going home and just about everything else.

"So you see, I shouldn't go to dinner, but it's not about you. I have to keep working on this," she finished. She didn't sound very convincing, though, even to herself. "I have to do whatever it takes to keep this place going."

"Well, you have to eat."

"Gideon—"

"Why don't you let me help you at least finish the bells? Then we can see?"

Calla considered. Why was she being so stubborn about this?

"I…guess. I mean, if you really want to, I wouldn't say no. They seem to like you."

She looked out at the crowd—noticing the appreciative looks several women closer to the window were giving Gideon.

"I'd better bring out some samples."

"I can do it, if you like."

"Um, sure."

She put together a tray and let him take it out. She noticed he grabbed a stack of the business cards she kept on the counter and took those as well, handing one out with each sample.

Why hadn't she ever thought of that?

She continued to work as he chatted with the group and eventually came back in with an empty tray.

"You received rave reviews, as usual," he said. "And I had an idea."

"What's that?"

"Why don't you let them decide on whether you should go to dinner with me tonight?"

"What?"

"Make them feel more involved. We can ask them if you should go to dinner with me."

"Are you saying we should take a vote?" Her voice rose slightly, incredulous.

"Why not? Maybe if you can find more ways to get them involved each day, you'll draw more and more people. That's the point, right?"

Calla narrowed her eyes. "Are you sure you're a cop?"

He grinned. "My sister's in marketing."

"I see. That was a good move with the business cards. But I think I can make up my own mind about dinner. If we can get enough work done, I think it would be nice. Thank you."

And I might not say no to anything else you have in mind, either.

Not that she would throw herself at him again only to be rebuffed—she'd had enough of that—but…her eyes drifted down to his hands.

Gideon grinned, sitting back down after washing his hands again.

"You already told them to vote yes, didn't you?" Calla intuited, and saw his smile widen.

She felt the responding smile tug at the edges of her lips, her mood lightening somewhat. It was kind of nice to have someone to talk to as she worked. She hadn't shared a kitchen with anyone for a few years, and she'd missed it. Or maybe it was Gideon's company in particular that was so nice.

"What about your own family? Don't you need to be home for the holiday?" she asked.

He returned to his bell, finishing it up before walking to the freezer to grab another hunk of cake.

"No, not this year. That's part of why I offered to help Nathan out. My mother passed away over the summer, unexpectedly. My sister invited me to her place in Arizona for the holiday, but honestly, it was easier to get away. I've never seen New York at Christmas, so I figured, why not?"

"I'm so sorry to hear about your mom. You were close?"

"We were. She raised us alone—my dad died in the line of duty when we were kids, so you know how it is."

Calla swallowed hard. She did know, sort of. Her family had had their own share of close calls.

"I do. Dad was almost killed in an accident when I was twelve, and I lived in fear every time he left the house after that. For Nathan, Bill and Gina, too, for that matter."

Gideon frowned. "Is that why you left? Too much worry?"

Calla looked up sharply. "I didn't leave. I went to school, which happened to be here in New York. But yes, I suppose it was nice to be in an environment where I didn't have to think about the danger they were in every day or listen to all of the police and fire reports over dinner every night."

"Not to mention how much of a pain in the butt it had to be when your older brothers were all cops, too," Gideon said with a grin, lightening the mood. "Had to make dating tough."

She rolled her eyes, laughing. "You have no idea."

She and Gideon worked and chatted for a few more hours, until the skies outside the shop window darkened. When Calla got up to stretch her legs, she saw it was snowing like crazy out.

"I still love seeing the snow," she said. "We got some in Texas now and then, but not like this."

Gideon joined her at the window.

"This is the first snow I've ever seen—real snow, not the slushy Texas stuff," he said.

Calla turned to him in surprise. "Really? You've never seen snow?"

He shook his head, staring out the window in awe that made the young boy in him shine through.

"Not like this."

Her heart warmed. "Well, then, what are we doing in here?" She opened the door and went outside.

He joined her just in time for her to smack him in the side of the head with a makeshift snowball. The snow was soft and fluffy, so no harm done. Calla laughed at his momentary shock, and then at the sheer glee in his expression as he scooped up some snow and threw it back at her.

He managed to get her at the back of her neck, and the snow slid down her back, making her wiggle as the cold snaked down her spine.

"Oh, good shot, but so cold," she said, still laughing and shivering at the same time.

Then she caught his eye, how he watched her, and she stopped wiggling. Gideon's dark hair was plastered against his forehead, wet from the snow, his cheeks ruddy from the cold. The look he leveled at her, though, was hot enough to make her forget the icy snow sliding down her back.

For a moment, so much heat leaped between them they might as well have been back behind the barn in midsummer rather than standing in the middle of a snowstorm.

Then he broke the connection, shaking the snow from his dark hair as he turned to go back inside.

Oh, no, you don't.

Turnabout was fair play, and Calla hadn't grown up with two older brothers without knowing how to hold her own. She scooped up some snow, quickly catching up with him as he walked back into the store. She grabbed the back of his sweater, dropping the icy bundle down inside.

His yelp was her reward.

When he spun around, wiggling as she had, she grinned and closed the distance between them.

"Wait. I know a better way to warm you up," she said, pushing up on tiptoe and kissing him.

She meant it to be a quick kiss—or maybe she didn't. Calla was exhausted, thrown off her game by the strange week and by being so close to Gideon for most of the day.

All she could think about while they'd been making those wedding bells was the kiss she'd had with him nearly a decade ago.

She'd wondered if it would be as good now.

It wasn't. It was better.

His lips were still cool from the outdoors, firm and just right. She darted her tongue out to taste him and his arms came around her, pulling her up tight against him. She slid her hands under his sweater to flatten her palms against his solid—and slightly wet—back. Gideon took over the kiss almost without her realizing it, parting her lips wider as his tongue made all kinds of promises to hers.

Calla moaned and pressed her hips into his, and then again as his erection nudged against her belly through his slacks.

"If you need to keep an eye on me, this is a much better way, I'd say," she whispered into his ear.

As soon as she said the words, Gideon's hold loosened, and he backed away.

"I'm sorry, Calla. I shouldn't have done that."

She blinked, still not quite recovered from his touch. "Why not? And technically, by the way, I did *that* to you."

"I thought after so much time we wouldn't have the same chemistry, or I…I don't know what I thought."

She frowned. "But we do have it. And what's wrong with it? Unless…" Her stomach dropped as she realized what could be the very large problem. "You have someone back home?"

She'd never thought he might be attached, even married. Her eyes dropped to his left hand. No ring. But that didn't mean anything these days. A lot of people she knew were in committed relationships without the traditional symbols.

"Absolutely not. There's no one."

Her knees almost sagged with relief.

"Except your brother Nathan."

Calla froze, momentarily stunned.

"My brother? Wait. No. I know for a fact he's been seeing a woman he's fairly serious about for the last year—"

Gideon rolled his eyes. "No, not like that. Jeez. I mean, he's my *friend,* and he asked me to come here to see if you were okay, not get you into bed. I'm fairly sure doing that breaks some kind of code that would allow him to shoot me if he found out."

Calla read between the lines as fast as Gideon spoke.

"But you'd be interested otherwise?"

"I'm so interested I'll be using a lot of cold water back at my hotel tonight."

"So…" Calla posited what seemed to be the obvious thought. "Why does he have to find out? What business is it of his?"

"You think he wouldn't know if I was seeing his younger sister?"

"I'm not talking about a long-term relationship, Gideon. I'm not moving back to Texas, and I assume you aren't planning to move to New York, so…why not enjoy each other's company for the holidays? I can show you the city, and you can make sure no bad men attack me."

"I think I would be the bad man attacking you," he said dryly, but she could also see he was interested.

"Sounds good to me."

In part, Calla almost couldn't believe the words coming out of her own mouth, but the more she spoke, the more she convinced herself, if not Gideon.

This was the perfect way to spend her Christmas holiday. A few days of no-strings mattress gymnastics with Gideon was suddenly all she wanted for Christmas.

Then he shook his head. "If he asked, I'd have to tell him the truth, and it could ruin a good friendship. Not to mention the trust we have on the job. You know that trust is a serious thing."

She couldn't argue the point. The wind went out of Calla's sails as she realized she'd done the exact thing she'd promised herself she wouldn't do—she'd thrown herself at Gideon again, only to have him walk away.

She felt like an idiot. Humiliated twice by the same guy. Wouldn't she ever learn?

"Fine. You're absolutely right, and I understand. So, if you don't mind, I'm going to close up for the night. Your help was great. Thank you," she added stiffly. "You can ask the police anything you want. The detective in charge was Howser. I hope you have a nice trip back."

With that, she walked to the door and held it open in a clear message for him to leave. The cold air rushing in reminded her of how hot he'd gotten her minutes before, adding to her resolve. If he was going to walk away this time, she was making sure it was at her invitation.

Gideon blew out a breath. "Calla, please—"

"Really, I do understand, Gideon. Have a safe trip."

When he halted his progress, pausing next to her by the door, she thought for one hopeful second that he'd changed his mind. That he might sweep her up and say the heck with her brother, but he only looked at her one more time with regret and then stepped out the door into the snow.

Calla shut the door behind him, locked it and went back to work on her cake. She'd lied about going home to sleep. Right now the last thing she wanted was to go to bed alone.

3

GIDEON KNEW HE'D done the right thing—just as he'd done by walking away eight years ago.

Doing the right thing sucked, but it was a lesson his father had drilled into him when he was very young.

He wished he could have broken the rules this once. But Nathan wasn't just another cop on the force; he was Gideon's partner. Nate had trained him, and they'd worked together ever since. He'd saved Gideon's life, and the trust they shared wasn't something Gideon took lightly. Gideon was supposed to make sure Nate's sister was safe—not seduce her.

Calla's offer of a holiday affair had been torture to turn down, especially since he hadn't been with anyone in a while. On top of the demands of his job, his mom's death and the resulting grief, sex had been the last thing on his mind.

Until he'd seen Calla. Now it was all he could think about. She was right—who would know? Well, he would.

He entered the large double doors of the local precinct where Calla had reported her break-in, announcing his arrival at the reception desk.

Gideon looked at postings on a corkboard in the hall for a few minutes, waiting.

"Detective Stone?"

An older guy, short and squat, but no less tough for his stockier stature, stood behind him. Gideon could tell Detective Howser had been in the game for a while. He'd probably seen it all, and more.

"Detective Howser. Call me Gideon. Thanks for taking a minute to talk to me."

"Sure, no problem," the detective responded with a thick

New York accent, waving Gideon on to follow him back to his office.

Inside, he shut the door. "What can I do for you, Tex?"

Gideon grinned, not minding the moniker the detective casually threw his way. "I wondered if you could give me any more information on an attempted robbery that happened four days ago at a bakery in Chelsea…"

Awhile later, Gideon emerged from the precinct resolved not to leave the city, or Calla. Not just yet, anyway.

The fingerprints taken from the knife belonged to a repeat offender with a long rap sheet—one that included several assaults as well as robberies and other crimes. He'd done two stints in prison already, and tended to hold a grudge. Gideon's gut was telling him it wasn't time to head back to Texas just yet. Howser had said they were scouring the neighborhoods to turn him up. Once Gideon knew the police had the thief in custody, then he could relax and consider his work done. However, Calla wasn't exactly going to welcome him back into her shop, or her life.

Returning to her shop in his rental car, he drove by to check that she was in the store, working—she was. He found himself some coffee and a sandwich, and then parked in a spot down the street from the shop, under a snow-covered tree. The streets were busy. She didn't know his car, and Gideon was good enough not to be spotted tailing her—and to spot anyone else who might be following her, as well.

He settled in, watching Calla's storefront. From a distance. Which was exactly as it should be. He had no place coming on to or kissing Calla Michaels. This was the price he'd pay for getting too close in the first place.

It made for a long afternoon and evening. Calla didn't even leave to get dinner; she worked straight through, sitting at her table. The crowd in front of the shop seemed a bit larger today.

Did Calla's family have any clue what amazing work she was doing, and the effort she put into it? When Nathan had said she ran a bakery, Gideon had pictured doughnuts and Italian bread, but what Calla did was as much art as baking. Clearly as dedicated as she was talented, she easily worked the same kind of hours that he—or any of her family members—did.

He needed to stretch his legs and got out of the car to take a turn around the neighborhood while keeping an eye on the shop. It was considerably less busy this time of night, when Calla's Cakes was one of the last businesses open.

Shortly after midnight, the lights in the shop turned off and Calla finally emerged from the front door. She'd mentioned that her apartment was within walking distance when they'd been chatting in the bakery. Gideon locked his car and followed on foot.

He'd make sure she was safely tucked inside for the night, then he could come back and move the car to a spot near her home. So much for the pricey hotel room he'd booked, but this was the job. It was going to be a long, cold night, he thought as he pulled his coat around him, keeping a safe distance behind Calla from the opposite side of the street.

She walked with the crisp step he saw other New Yorkers use, moving through the dark street to her destination as if completely focused on that task alone. The area seemed safe enough—still, it was late, and she was alone.

Five minutes later, she turned to climb the stairs toward the wrought iron doors of an older brick apartment building. There was a decorated tree on one side of the yard, and a menorah across the walk. Several tenants had decorated their windows as well, making it very cheerful and bright. Near the top, Calla slipped her hand inside her bag for her keys.

The next few seconds were a blur. Everything happened so fast that Gideon was unprepared when he saw a shadow dart out and grab Calla from behind, dragging her back down the steps and into a small courtyard.

Gideon was across the street in seconds, reaching for his

gun—which he didn't have, and wasn't allowed to carry, in the city. That didn't stop him, though.

Dashing into the darkness where the intruder had dragged Calla, Gideon called her name and heard her muffled reply. Someone was covering her mouth. He saw them scuffling in the corner under a barren tree and ran in that direction, taking the attacker by the back of his coat collar and pulling.

"Get off her!" Gideon growled. Primal emotion ran through him as he yanked the man back from Calla, and then… extreme pain made him gasp.

Hollers of agony filled the quiet courtyard. A tenant in the building yelled something from a window up above them. Gideon was knocked back on his butt into the snow. Someone fell on top of him—the attacker? He couldn't see; his eyes were on fire. He grasped for something, an arm, a leg, but there was nothing.

"Calla? Where are you? Are you okay?" Gideon pushed himself up from the wet ground and saw a blurry image of Calla appear in his view.

"I'm right here, Gideon, where did you come from? Oh, my, I'm so sorry, look at you, let's get inside…"

He could feel her shaking as she took his hand, her voice desperate. Afraid. Gideon shook his head, knowing better than to rub his eyes, though he wanted to do so desperately.

"Where is he?"

"He ran off. I sprayed him at the same time you pulled him away from me. I didn't know you were right there, and I got you, too. I'll call a cab to get to the ER."

"No, that's not necessary. I need some water, please."

He could see, more or less, out of one eye; the other was worse. She led him up three flights of stairs, repeating that she was so, so sorry as they went. Once inside her small apartment, she led him to the kitchen.

"Do you have any grease-fighting detergent?" he asked.

"Yes, my dish soap."

"Could you put some in a large bowl, very diluted?"

He watched her bustle around the kitchen with his one good eye, the burning in the other almost unbearable. When she put the bowl in front of him, he closed his eyes and pushed his face into the soapy water for as long as he could, then came out, rinsed under a clean spray in the sink, and repeated the process.

"A towel?"

She pushed one into his hand and he dried off, starting to breathe more easily as the pain subsided.

"Damn it, that stuff hurts," he said, leaning back against the wall, opening his eyes slowly. "Can you replace that soapy water with some new so I can do it again?"

"Sure. Is it helping?"

"Yes, very much. It's the only thing that can dissolve the oils in the pepper spray from your skin—you just have to be careful to keep them from running back into your eyes when you rinse."

"I see. Well, if it helps at all, I think the guy who grabbed me got the most of it."

"Good."

Gideon rinsed his face and eyes again, and after a half hour of doing so, felt considerably better. Thank goodness civilian-issue pepper spray was a lot weaker than the type they used on the force, which could burn your skin and even irritate your lungs. This was bad enough.

He looked at Calla, who hadn't taken her coat off yet. She was pale, with deep shadows under her eyes. Her obvious concern only accentuated them. As his vision cleared, he also noticed a scrape on her hand as she lifted it to remove the bowl from the counter, and there was a light bruise forming on her cheek.

His fury at the idea of someone hurting her far outweighed the lingering sting of the pepper spray.

"Was it the same guy? Did you see him?"

She shook her head. "I don't know. He stayed behind me, though his voice sounded the same, but I was so frightened and it all happened so fast."

"Let me see," he said, stepping forward and taking her hand in his, looking at the scrape and then putting his hand under her jaw. He touched the bruise gently and was relieved to find it rubbed away, only a smudge of grime.

It didn't make him any less angry.

He started to pull his hand away, but hers rose to cover it. "Thank you for being there. I'm so sorry I got you with the spray."

Her voice shook, and a tear slipped down her cheek. Gideon groaned, pulling her in close and holding her until she stopped shaking.

"He's probably regretting grabbing you tenfold right now. Good for you for thinking fast and being able to use the spray. I only wish I'd seen him sooner." He lowered his lips to kiss her soft dark hair. "Do you want me to look at that scrape?"

She shook her head. "It's no big deal. I need to clean up, though. I'll be fine."

Tough, smart, strong. Calla could take care of herself, but it didn't stop Gideon from wanting to help.

"It was possibly your attacker from the store—unlike a lot of criminals, this one has a history of coming back for more. The NYPD should have told you that. We have to report this."

"I will, in the morning. He's probably long gone now, and it might not even have been him. I can't be sure. I'm so tired. I really need to clean up and sleep."

Gideon believed it. She looked ready to fall asleep on her feet.

"Okay. You do that. Lock the doors. I'll be outside if you need me. Hand me your cell phone so I can give you my number." Gideon planned on talking to Howser as soon as he left. If the attacker was suffering from being sprayed, he'd be slowed down and blinded, perhaps seeking help—the perfect time to catch him.

She blinked up at him, frowning. "Outside? Why would you be outside?"

"I know you don't want me around, but I'm not leaving, or letting you out of my sight, until we know this guy is caught."

Realization dawned in her expression. "You were watching me."

"I talked to the detective on your case, and he filled me in on some disturbing details about this guy. I couldn't leave without knowing you were okay. It's no big deal. It's my job."

She looked up at him, a little less blurry. "It's a big deal to me. Thank you."

Gideon didn't expect that—he expected her to be ticked off—so he was surprised at her thanks.

"Um, sure. Listen, why don't you take that shower, and I'm going to call this in."

There was a breath of silence between them, and she looked up at him. "Why don't you call it in and then join me in the shower?"

Gideon's heart tripped over itself, his body hardening almost instantaneously. Before he could object, she cut in again.

"I seem to be making a habit of throwing myself at you," she said with a slight smile. "But I really don't want to be alone right now, Gideon. Please don't leave again."

Damn it. Of all the appeals she might have made, that one socked him in the gut.

"Please," she whispered, lifting up and pressing a kiss to his mouth.

She continued kissing him until he gave in, unable to resist a deeper taste. Gideon knew he wouldn't be walking away from Calla again that night.

CALLA'S FEARS WERE forgotten as soon as she felt Gideon relent, his body relaxing as he pulled her in closer, his mouth finding hers again. They took their time now, getting to know each other, understanding that there was no need to rush.

"I guess I could use a shower, too," he said against her mouth, making her smile. "After I make this call."

"Okay. Don't be long."

She waited for him to report the attack, watching the way his expression changed, and his voice, as he talked to the other detective. It made him look dangerous. And even sexier. Calla waited until he was done—she didn't want to give him a chance to change his mind.

When he hung up, she took him by the hand, leading him back to her bedroom. She stopped by the bed, removed her coat, and started taking everything else off, as well. He watched with rapt attention.

Guilt assailed her as she took in the puffy redness still apparent around his eyes and on his cheeks. Down to her bra and panties, she stepped forward, framing his face with her hands.

"Does it still hurt?"

"Are you kidding? My eyes are the happiest they've ever been right now," he said with a lopsided smile that warmed her heart.

His fingers slid around to the back of her bra, unclasping it and letting it fall loose. Calla shrugged it to the floor, inviting his gaze. She wasn't self-conscious about her body, and she could tell from the heat in his eyes that he liked what he saw.

"You're way overdressed for the shower," she said, reaching to push his sweater up over his head, and then the T-shirt under it.

She wasn't disappointed, but she'd known she wouldn't be. Leaning in, she darted her tongue out to follow along the smooth edge of one sculptured muscle and smiled when he groaned.

"Calla…"

The way he said her name was a caution and a promise.

She reached for his belt buckle, but he backed away, quickly shucking his pants himself.

Calla caught her breath as she took him in. No, she wasn't disappointed in any way whatsoever.

"You keep looking at me like that and we're never making it into the shower."

"That would be a shame. I can think of all kinds of fun we'll have in there."

Sliding her panties to the floor, she walked ahead and let him watch her, putting a little extra swing in her step as she went into the en suite and turned on the light. Her heart was racing as she stepped in under the steamy spray and waited for him to join her.

Was this finally really happening? Did she actually have Gideon Stone naked in a shower with her? He tugged her under the water with him, his mouth landing on hers in a hard, hot kiss.

Definitely real.

Calla closed her fingers over his erection jutting against her hip and stroked. He broke the kiss on a heavy groan, burying his face in her neck. She enjoyed how he pushed into her hand in a needy rhythm.

Then his hands were on her, too, dipping in between her thighs as he moved his lips down her shoulder to her breast, sucking a nipple into his mouth as his fingers did devilish things between her legs.

"Oh, Gideon," She sighed, wanting more than his fingers.

Luckily, he wanted the same thing, and hiked her leg up by his hip, backing her against the tile wall under the spray.

"Protection?" he managed as he nibbled at her lips. His hips pressed seductively against hers, making her moan as he teased her clit with the broad head of his shaft.

"Oh, right," she gasped, thankful he remembered. "Lemme…"

She disengaged herself from this delightful position and

reached out to the vanity, where she opened a drawer and reached in to get a small foil packet.

Good to go.

Ripping it open, she sank to her knees in the shower and before she applied it, let herself enjoy one more luxury as she closed her lips over him instead. Her body went into overdrive at the sensation of his wet, velvety skin against her tongue, pressing into the back of her throat.

"Stop," he commanded brusquely. She knew why and let him pull her up again as her hands deftly covered him.

This time he positioned her face-first against the tile, her hands braced as he widened her stance from behind.

"Okay?" he asked softly, against her ear.

"More than," she managed, levering her hips back slightly in invitation.

He took that invitation as he nudged against her, experimenting, and then entering her body deeply until they were both gasping with the intensity of it. Calla had never felt so turned on—at the same time, she felt so safe and supported as his arms came around her.

His hands covered her breasts as he started to move, gently strumming his fingers over her tender skin. He whispered hot endearments in her ear in between kisses along the back of her neck.

Calla couldn't form words, only sounds, as he picked up the pace, thrusting faster while covering her hands with his against the wall, their fingers entwining. Her body welcomed him, clutching and wanting more. She rolled her hips in rhythm with his thrusts until they were both crying out, their bodies pulsing together in a long, hard climax.

Calla lost track of time, of how long they stood there, joined, wringing every last second of pleasure from each other. All she knew, as he turned her to him and slid his hands into her wet hair as he kissed her, was that she wanted more.

4

GIDEON HAD TRAVELED a bit, usually in connection with his job, but he'd never fallen for a city like he did for New York. Or maybe it was the woman who lived here, but suddenly the bleakness of the past few months faded, making everything magical again.

He sat in the corner of the bakery studio reading as Calla worked on building and decorating the bell cake for the gathering of people outside. She'd built a clever trellis to arrange the bells on, her ingenuity captivating him. She was clever in and out of bed, he thought with a smile.

And just as thorough.

Everyone knew that the decorated windows were a huge draw in the city this time of year, but he found it hard to believe that anything could match watching Calla work.

Well, except for watching Calla stretch sensuously beneath him, her hair scattered over a pillow as he planted himself deep inside her body, but that wasn't for public consumption.

Looking past her, he realized that nothing here was decorated. Nothing in her apartment had been, either. Not even a wreath on the door or lights in the window.

Calla was having a difficult time drawing attention to her business. The shop was surviving, but barely, she'd confided. She was even considering moving out of her apartment to save money for the bakery, living here in her office until things picked up.

Gideon admired her determination, but he hoped things wouldn't go to that extreme. Her shop space was nice, but not livable. He thought of all the nights he'd stayed overnight at the station, sleeping on the couch in his small office or even at his desk, but that was different. Some cases took a long time to settle. Calla was thinking about giving up her living space just to save her business. There had to be another way.

He walked back into Calla's office to make a phone call to his sister. After explaining the situation, he hoped he could get some ideas of how to help Calla, and he did. Now the trick would be to convince her to go along with it.

Calla had gone outside, handing out samples, and he was glad to see her chatting a bit with the group. And giving them her business cards. She'd listened to him about connecting with her audience.

But what made them come back every day? What made them want more?

Gideon had an idea, but he wasn't sure Calla would like it. She was so hardworking, but that dedication to her work, along with the worry about her business, created so much stress that she was missing out on the fun. People saw her work hard, but that's all they saw. Maybe he could help show them something more—what he saw in her.

When she came back in, her cheeks rosy from the cold, he took a dollop of icing on his finger and dabbed it to her nose before she could sit back down.

"Gideon! What—"

He grabbed a towel from the counter as he pulled her toward him with the other hand. But instead of wiping the frosting from her nose, he caught it with his tongue and then pressed his mouth to hers in a gentle, sweet kiss—literally sweet as they shared the frosting.

For a moment, heat leaped between them as Calla melted against him before remembering where they were. She pulled away, looking scandalized.

"Gideon!"

She had no need to worry. The crowd, as they often said, went wild. Applause and cheers met them from the half dozen or so people who had witnessed the kiss.

"The wedding cake lady has a boyfriend!" someone said.

"And he's hot!" another voice chimed in.

Gideon grinned and Calla looked struck dumb.

The look she gave him wasn't a friendly one.

"What do you think you're doing?" she hissed under her breath.

"Just go with it," he said in her ear.

Calla slid Gideon a look as she promptly closed the shades.

"Gideon—"

"Calla," he said at the same time, and they both stopped. He smiled; she sighed.

Gideon crossed over to her and put his hands on her shoulders.

"Hear me out. When you were working, I had an idea. I called my sister to ask her about how you could do some marketing, and I told her how you work in the window."

"Yeah?"

Gideon nodded, encouraged at the flicker of interest in her expression. And the satisfied flush in her cheeks from his kiss.

"Yes. She said the performance baking is good, but people can't necessarily connect with it."

"I don't understand—who can't connect with cake? And weddings?"

"That's true, but what you do is really about romance. Happily ever afters, right? And yet your storefront isn't making that connection. Giving them something to relate to, and something to root for."

"Or looking like someone who seems completely unprofessional."

"I doubt that, not when they see how hard you work. Diedre said that you need to do something that could really draw attention. You have to admit, that kiss drew some attention."

"I still don't get it, and I can't see how this will make people buy more cakes."

"Because it will get them talking—to others at work, or at home—and it will bring them back. My mother was telling me about coffee commercials they ran back in the eighties, I think, where each commercial was like a story over coffee. People wanted to watch the commercials to see what happened—and then they bought the coffee because they liked the story. If people watch you and make the connection between what you do and romance, that's stronger than just seeing how hard you work."

Gideon could feel her tension, and turned her around and massaged her tight shoulders as he leaned in closer and kissed her neck.

"Gideon," she moaned in half pleasure, half protest, but she didn't move away. "I have to finish the cake."

"You need to learn to relax a little, Calla."

"There's no time. And we relaxed a lot, all last night."

He laughed against the back of her neck.

"Listen, why don't you leave this to me? Let me try a few things, and let's see what works?"

"Oh, I don't know…"

Gideon nibbled on her ear, loving her taste. Sweet like the sugar she used on the cakes.

"Trust me, Calla. What can it hurt?"

She groaned as he sucked the tender skin under her ear, and Gideon was starting to lose focus, as well.

"I have to get to work," she protested lamely, but didn't pull away.

"In a minute."

Gideon had a taste of her and he wanted more before he had to let her go back into her world. He left her only to lock the door before returning, wrapping his arms around her from behind, undoing the buttons of her chef's coat, sliding his hands underneath.

Good thing she'd pulled the shades.

She arched back against him, catching her breath as his hands closed over her breasts, teasing.

"Sex produces endorphins, you know...it will help with your energy levels," he whispered in her ear before biting the lobe lightly.

"I can't have sex in here. It's against health codes."

"Right, we'll be careful about that," he said gruffly as he worked his hands up under her blouse, loving the warm silk of her skin.

She chuckled softly against his mouth as he kissed her again. Gideon walked her back to the small office. Inside, he eyed the desk.

"No health-code violations in here, right?"

"That's true," she admitted, letting him draw her inside.

Gideon couldn't wait another second to kiss her—to really kiss her—and he loved how she deftly undid his belt, running her fingers over his stomach.

When her hands slipped inside his jeans to touch him, he caught his breath, his head falling forward to her shoulder. He was hard as a rock already, and she murmured her approval in her ear as she nipped his earlobe and stroked him gently.

Gideon was sure he'd never felt so much with anyone before in his life. Calla's touch turned him inside out.

He darted his tongue out to taste the smooth skin of her shoulder and raised a hand to cover her breast, stroking her there in the same rhythm she did for him. She trembled as her nipple hardened under his fingers, and she sought a kiss that he was more than willing to give.

Gideon thought about taking her on the desk, which was still a possibility, but he didn't want to break the intimacy of the kiss or the touches they were sharing, even though he was increasingly close to embarrassing himself.

Calla seemed to know, backing away from the kiss, breathless, her cheeks flushed, eyes bright.

"Touch me, too," she said, before fusing her mouth to his again.

Her wish was his command. Bringing her a little closer, he slid his hand up the firm muscle of her thigh under her skirt. She'd worn tights in the winter cold, but he got them out of the way and eased his fingers inside the scrap of lace she wore under them.

"Oh, yes." She sighed as his fingers stroked her sex, her slick skin telling him how ready she was.

It had been a lot of years since he'd done anything like this, kissing and getting off with a woman just by touching. It was wildly hot.

"You're so soft," he murmured against her cheek as he felt his body tighten, close to release. He wanted to last, but she was a devil with those hands, not letting him escape the rising tide.

He captured the hard tip of her breast with his lips through her blouse as he moved one finger inside her, then two, thrusting into her heat and drawing a long moan from her.

"Oh, Gideon, yes…"

The way she said his name and surged against him was all he could take. Pleasure rushed from him, the orgasm stealing his breath as his body moved against her of its own volition. He gladly let it steal his sanity for the next few moments.

She cried out, too, seconds later, her head dropping back, her face a study in sheer pleasure as she rode out her release. Gideon kissed her throat, tried to catch his breath as he brought her closer, holding her against him for several long minutes.

Calla snuggled into him, warm and relaxed as she sighed in contentment against his shoulder. Gideon was a bit shaken, for reasons he couldn't understand. He'd intended on having some fun, doing something spontaneous. What had just passed between them was, instead, unbearably intimate—more so than he would have expected for a quick office interlude.

Maybe it was the residual afterglow, but he felt closer to Calla than he had to anyone he could remember in recent memory. The fact was that he was feeling things he'd never expected to feel—or maybe he'd known all along. Maybe he'd known when he first kissed her back at the barn, and that was why he'd walked away.

Because Calla could never be casual. She was so much more than that.

He wasn't so sure that she felt the same way about him.

"I—I should wash up and get back to work," she said, almost apologetically, straightening her clothing.

"You do that. I'm going to go do a few things. It won't take long. Call me if you need me," he said, leaning in for a long, soft kiss.

"As if there's any question."

Surprise flickered in his brain at her response, and he wasn't sure what to say, so he didn't say anything. With a smile, he left the office, checking to make sure everything was secure before he left.

Now he had to set a plan in motion, to romance Calla in her bakery window and hope that it not only saved her shop, but convinced her that maybe they were more than a holiday fling, as well.

It started with the Christmas lights.

Gideon had returned to the shop with his arms chock-full of Christmas lights. He'd insisted that she needed to decorate her shop and her window and door.

Calla found it impossible to work with him crawling all over the place hanging lights and decorations, so she'd done the inevitable—she'd given in and helped.

Surprisingly, many of the people walking home from work or out strolling with their dogs had stopped to watch, applauding with oohs and ahhs when Gideon turned the lights on.

Then he pulled a piece of mistletoe out of his pocket and held it over her head for a kiss.

This one she granted him happily. The shop did look more in the holiday spirit, and it made Calla feel so, as well.

"Thank you, Gideon. This is lovely. I didn't have time to decorate, but so many people are stopping to look at the lights."

He nodded, clearly excited. He was so sweet, she thought, her heart warm.

"And did you notice what I put over in this window? They're noticing that right along with it."

She'd been working on the other side of the shop, and hadn't seen what he'd been up to. Letting him lead her outside, eyes closed, she opened them when he said and was struck by what she found.

Twelve color pictures from her website of some of the most elaborate cakes she'd made that year hung in the window, all framed with lights.

"Gideon…this is…awesome."

"I thought so, too. How could someone not want one of your cakes? The website address is listed at the bottom of each one, too."

Calla shook her head, barely feeling the cold as she stared at her bright, lively windows. The pictures were definitely eye-catching from the sidewalk, and even from the street.

"You're brilliant. How could I have missed putting pictures of cakes in the window? I have the catalog in here on the counter, but I never considered this."

"Well, it was one of Diedre's ideas, and she is brilliant. You can't think of everything, Calla. You have a lot to deal with here, making these cakes."

"Remind me to send your sister a thank-you. This is very sweet, Gideon," she said again, feeling a little choked up.

Calla had felt alone in her career since she'd started out. While she had friends, they were also often her competitors.

Her family was far away, and supported her in a general sense, but not like this. No one had ever done anything like this for her. Even as she stood there, people stopped to check out the window and pointed to which cakes they liked best.

They went back inside, and Calla turned to Gideon, giving him a spontaneous hug. It didn't matter to her if anyone was watching.

"I did have fun today. I'll have to get here a little earlier tomorrow to finish, but this really was wonderful."

"I'm glad," he said, loosening the bun she'd pulled her hair back into and running his fingers through it in a way that lit up her nerve endings as brightly as the shop.

"Maybe we could get some dinner and head back to my place?"

"Sounds great. I'm starving," he said with a chuckle, backing away.

Calla missed his touch when he let go. Oh, no. That wasn't good. She had to be tired—she was feeling far more warm and fuzzy than she should. This was only a fling, only sex. And Gideon was just being nice, helping her with the shop.

"Me, too, really," she said with a smile, closing up and grabbing her coat. "It's been a long time since lunch."

As they walked out onto the street, Gideon didn't let go of her hand.

"So, you know the city and the food better than I do. Any preference?"

"It's too late for a lot of restaurants if we don't have reservations, especially this time of year, but I have a friend who runs a small place in Spanish Harlem where you can get the best burrito in the city."

"Better than that place on Rudd St. in Houston?"

"Oh, man, way better," she said, rolling her eyes. "No comparison."

She knew the spot he meant; it was one of the places cops

ate regularly because it was open all night. It had a decent menu for a take-out place, but nothing like Diego's.

"Let's go, then," he said jovially.

"We should take a cab—it's in East Harlem, and probably not a place you want to leave your rental car," she said, letting go of his hand as she stepped to the curb and hailed a taxi with an earsplitting whistle.

The yellow cab appeared at the curb, screeching to a halt.

"Wow," Gideon said, holding the door for her as they got in. "That was impressive. I tried to grab one a few times today, and it took me three tries."

"It depends on the time of day, the weather, and if they are on duty or not. And a good strong whistle doesn't hurt. One of the useful things my brothers taught me to do."

Gideon was sure a nice pair of legs helped, too.

The ride was fast and furious, and Calla let Gideon keep her close in the back of the cab. Far too soon, the cabbie pulled up to the curb again.

"Are you sure this is it?" Gideon asked, looking around as they paid and got out of the cab.

Calla laughed and took his arm. "Yes, quite sure."

A short ways down the street, she turned him into an alley and opened a door on the side, where the spicy scents of peppers and cumin met them and made her mouth water.

"Awesome, there's a table open," she said, grabbing his arm and pulling him toward a corner in the back.

The small cantina was crowded and alive with chatter as they claimed what seemed to be the last table in the place. Calla slid up onto the raised seat, victorious.

"I wouldn't have expected this from the outside," Gideon said, looking around in appreciation at the warm brick walls decorated with authentic Mexican textiles and other art. "It smells like heaven in here."

"There are a lot of places like this in the city. Real estate is expensive and hard to come by, so small hidden gems like this are everywhere."

"And you know the owner?"

"Yes. Diego is the head chef, as well. He grew up in this neighborhood."

As soon as she said it, her friend appeared at the edge of the kitchen and spotted her. He smiled, heading directly toward her. Calla met him halfway with a hearty hug.

"Calla, what a wonderful surprise."

"I have a friend visiting from Texas. I couldn't let him leave the city without tasting your amazing burritos."

Calla lead Diego back to the table and she saw Gideon watching them, his eyes narrowed slightly, his jaw tight.

"Gideon, this is Diego Jones, the owner and the chef. And the guy who saved my butt in sauces back in school."

"Nice to meet you, Gideon," Diego said heartily, shaking Gideon's hand. "Dinner is on the house tonight. I got my hands on some fresh stone crab today, and I'm using it for late-night special burritos. Do you like seafood?"

Calla smiled. Diego was one of the warmest and most generous people she knew, and it came out in his personality and his cooking.

"A crab burrito?" Gideon said, somewhat skeptically.

Calla squeezed Diego's arm as she levered herself back up into her chair. "Trust me, you won't want to miss it."

"Bring it on, then," Gideon said with another slight smile.

"I hope you'll enjoy it. Calla, you need to not be such a stranger."

Diego kissed her cheek before being called by another table; he backed away with a smile.

"Believe me, you won't ever find any food like what you are about to have here. His combinations of flavors and textures are mind-blowing."

Gideon nodded. "You two seem…close."

"We are. I've always been more of a baker than a cook,

and I met Diego in a course on sauces. I was botching it entirely. He saved my bacon…or my sauce, I suppose. He spent a lot of time out of class helping me perfect my technique."

"For sauce?"

"Well, yeah, what else?"

"It certainly is a popular place," Gideon commented as a server delivered two huge, colorful margaritas to their table.

Calla watched him touch the glass, picking up a strange vibe. He was tense, suddenly quiet, and even a bit surly.

Was Gideon jealous?

And why did that idea make her have to fight a female sense of satisfaction? She and Gideon weren't an item. They weren't even in a relationship. In a few days he'd be gone.

She was probably imagining his reaction. He was very likely just tired.

"Calla? Are you okay?"

"Oh, yes, sorry. I was just thinking about this place. He doesn't even advertise, which is amazing," Calla said wistfully. "He has a terrific product, good food and word spreads about things like that."

"You have a terrific product, too. But he seems to cater to a local area, like you said. He grew up here. He can feed fifty people at a time, every night. You can only make one cake at a time. It's completely different."

"You're right. I lose perspective sometimes."

Like right now? It felt so good to confide in Gideon. To share her burdens and have someone's support. She could easily lose perspective if she didn't take care.

"It will work out. You're too talented for it not to," he added, pulling her hand up to his lips.

Calla shivered at the touch of his mouth on her skin, and relented.

"Probably a hundred talented chefs fail here every day," she said realistically.

"You won't be one of them," he said, holding her gaze and

flicking his tongue out to taste the back of her pinky finger. That scrambled her thoughts immediately.

Their food was delivered just in time to divert their attention and reset the magic of the evening. Calla was relieved, as she really didn't want this to end.

Not yet.

5

"So why is it, exactly, that you owe my brother?" Calla asked as they walked along a quiet side street back in midtown, under starry winter skies.

Her words made little puffs of vapor in the cold air, drawing Gideon's attention to her mouth. The edges of her lips canted upward in a half smile as her gaze landed on some snowmen built earlier in the day, lined up along the edge of the walk.

Gideon loved everything about her mouth. It was very expressive, betraying her thoughts and her emotions with a slight tilt in either direction, and it was generous with smiles. And kisses. Very wonderful, hot kisses. Before he answered her question, he pulled her around to face him and bent down to help himself to one, unable to wait.

She didn't seem to mind, pressing closer and parting her lips under his, still tasting of lime, tequila and savory spices from their dinner. Gideon didn't want to stop, but when she shivered in his arms, he wasn't sure if it was from desire or cold.

He broke the kiss but kept her close to him as they continued walking, his arm slung around her shoulders.

"He took a bullet for me," Gideon said, feeling the same knot curl in his chest that he usually did when he said the words out loud. It had been two years, but the memory was still fresh. "He saved my life."

Gideon still sometimes went to bed haunted by the image of Nathan falling to the pavement. He had taken down the shooter, and Nathan had been wearing a vest, but still.

Calla froze, gripping his hand tightly as she stared up into his face.

"You were there? When he was shot? He never told me that."

"We were checking the alleys after an armed assault on a store owner, but it seemed like the guy was long gone. He wasn't—in fact, I walked right by him. He came up behind me. He would have killed me there, on the spot, if Nathan hadn't come around the corner. He yelled before the guy could shoot me, but then the guy turned on Nathan. Worst night of my life, seeing him fall," Gideon said.

He apologized softly as he realized he was squeezing Calla's hand a bit too tightly. She made some incomprehensible noise as she tightened her hand on his again.

"He was okay. He had a vest on—we both did. But it's just luck that the bullet hit there. I took the guy down right after he fired, but still. If the shot hadn't hit the vest, Nate could have been killed. Because of my carelessness."

Calla paused, as if absorbing the news. Was she wondering why he'd missed the guy who had been hiding down a small side alley? Was she thinking that his miss could have gotten her brother killed?

"I'm so glad he saved you," she finally said, to his surprise.

Something in her voice, a husky note that seemed to glide over his skin, made him want to get her alone.

"Want to grab a cab back to my hotel instead of your place? I have this fancy room, huge bathtub, huge bed…hardly being used," he said as he ducked down to nibble at the curve of her ear.

"Oh, a hot bath sounds perfect." She sighed.

"Even better if we share?" he added.

"Definitely. Though I don't see any cabs in service here. There's a subway a block down."

She was already heading that way, leading him by the hand, and he was happy to follow. They caught the train heading downtown in time and took some seats on a corner, with only a dozen or so other passengers all minding their own business on the far side of the car.

The sway and rattle of the subway car sent a vibration through Gideon's body that only emphasized how turned on he was, and he pulled Calla closer, finding her mouth to let her know, too.

"How long?" he whispered roughly in her ear.

"Maybe ten minutes, if that," she said, sounding a little shaky herself.

He saw the pulse hammering in her throat, and let his gaze drift down over the flush in her cheeks, not from the cold. Meeting his look with one of her own, she turned into him, closer, sliding her hand up his thigh and under the flap of his coat, her hand settling over the distinct bulge in his slacks.

Gideon had to bite down to repress a moan, closing his eyes and burying his face in her hair as she touched him so slightly, yet made his entire body stiffen with need.

"You keep doing that, I won't make it off the train," he muttered against the soft skin of her neck.

"Don't worry, you're in good hands," she said with an evil chuckle, flicking her tongue against his ear as she continued to touch him just enough to set him on fire, but not enough to quench the blaze.

By the time the train reached their stop, Gideon could hardly think straight. He was the one pulling her along as they both raced to his hotel. In the elevator on the way to his room, he gave her a taste of her own medicine, pressing her into the wall and touching her as she had him…a light hand grazing over a hard nipple, a nudge of his thigh at the apex of hers. She was trembling, as was he, when the doors finally opened.

Entering the hotel room, Gideon let the door slam shut, his key card falling to the floor. He didn't bother with a light. They were a tangle of sleeves and pant legs, belts and shoes flung every which way until all he felt was her skin against his.

"Oh, yeah, that's it…" he said, holding as much of her against him as he could fit.

Now that he had her here and naked, the urgency diminished somewhat and he slid his hands over her back and up into her hair, steadying her head so that he could explore the recesses of her mouth as deeply as possible, robbing them both of normal breath for long moments.

"I'm dizzy," she gasped softly, breaking the kiss for a moment. Her fingernails bit into his shoulders as she clung to him, and Gideon tightened his arms around her.

"Don't worry, I won't let you fall," he promised, trailing more kisses from the back of her ear down her neck and shoulder, finally finding his way to her breasts.

"You're delicious," he said roughly, drawing one ripe tip into his mouth and then the other, until she was whimpering and slack in his arms.

"Gideon, please," she begged, and that undid him.

The small exclamation of surprise when he picked her up made him smile as he carried her to the large sofa in the main room. He set her down gently and turned on the light on the nearby table.

He wanted to see…everything.

She was flushed and rosy, her dark hair a gorgeous mess from his hands, her curves inviting him to touch some more. One knee fell to the side; he saw the slight shimmer of arousal glistening on her thigh and knew exactly what he wanted.

She watched him, letting him look, and didn't say a word as he fell to his knees beside her, sliding his hand up her leg until he discovered the slick heat that invited him in.

Making a little more room, he levered over her and settled in, his shoulders widening her, opening her even more intimately to his view. He took his time, looking, touching and finally tasting so slowly she cried out his name.

It urged him on, his tongue flickering over her hot, hard nub as his fingers danced in other delicate places. He let her move, but only so much, his weight and shoulders pinning her in place so that he could continue until she buckled under him. He kept touching and tasting as she tightened and then went hot and loose beneath him, her cries turning to soft moans and then sighs as the urgency ebbed.

He moved up to lie alongside her, holding her close as his lips found hers. She was pliant and warm, her eyes hazy.

Her hands were on him again as she watched him now, touching and repositioning herself over him so that the tables were turned.

"Do you have…?" she asked, standing up.

"Yeah, in the black bag on the bathroom counter. Over there," he indicated, hating that she had to leave, but enjoying the view as she walked across the room to retrieve the protection he'd almost left back in Houston, not anticipating a need.

He'd been so wrong. There was a seemingly unquenchable, intense need.

She returned quickly, covered him with a touch that nearly set him off all by itself, and then she was over him, taking him in, taking control.

He lay back and watched her move over him, taking in the way her body moved, the grace of her form, the way her lips parted and her eyes closed as the heat built between them.

He groaned as she tightened around him, his hands finding her hips in a reflex to urge her on, to set the pace. She leaned in, her nails scraping lightly over his chest as he thrust upward, meeting her rhythm, seeking more.

Harder.

Deeper.

Gideon tried to slow down, to make it last for both of them, but Calla had other ideas, not relenting for a second.

"Calla, honey, *oh*…" he managed, but his body and breath tightened, stealing any more words.

He opened his eyes to see the wash of pleasure in her expression at the same time he erupted, taking them both out of themselves and into each other for long, scorching seconds.

She collapsed down over his chest in the most delightful heap of woman he'd ever had his hands on. Closing his arms around her, he didn't say another word, not wanting to break the spell. This had to have been one of the best evenings of his life.

Calla lifted up first, crossing her arms over his chest and propping her chin on her fists as she regarded him with sleepy, satisfied eyes.

"You said you have a bathtub that fits two?"

A smile pulled at his lips, desire tugging elsewhere at the spark of heat in her suggestion.

"I do."

"A good, long, hot soak sounds perfect right now."

He rubbed his hands over the smooth length of her back, moving down to the curve of her hip to nestle her closer.

"That does sound nice, but this is pretty comfortable," he responded, nuzzling her cheek.

"We could get pretty comfortable in your bed, too, after we get out of the tub," she pointed out with a sexy arch of her eyebrow.

"Let's go," Gideon agreed enthusiastically, making her smile widely.

Laughing, they made their way to the bath.

"If you want to start the bath, I'll get glasses and the bottle of wine I picked up the other night."

"Perfect."

Gideon found the bottle of expensive Bordeaux out in the front room, still in the bag. He'd actually bought it to send to his sister for Christmas, but he could pick up another bottle later. There was a corkscrew on the small refrigerator near a tiny minibar, and he snagged two of the water glasses left there and returned to the bath. Calla had turned on only one light in the corner, letting the lights from the tub illuminate the rest of the room in softly changing colors.

"You're kidding me—it lights up, too?" Gideon said, setting down the glasses and joining her.

She grinned like a kid with her favorite toy. "These are amazing. I've always said I'd get one, when I can afford a house someday. They have the bubble jets and the heated sides with the chromotherapy lights. Heaven," she said as she accepted the glass of wine he handed her.

"Chromotherapy?" Gideon settled in, sliding around so that he was sitting next to her. The tub, regardless of its bells and whistles, was very comfortable for two, and the jets felt fantastic.

"You know, like aromatherapy heals with scents, chromotherapy can relax you with use of certain color spectrums."

"Ah, okay. Like the sunlamp my captain always uses in his office in the winter. He says it helps his mood, so believe me, we're all for it, since he's no fun in a bad mood." Gideon paused. "Well, he's really no fun anyway, but the light can't hurt."

Calla laughed, sipping her wine. "Yeah, something like that. I've seen them on TV and in the stores, but I've never had the chance to use one before. Now I know I definitely have to have one."

The way her eyes dimmed a little after she said that told him she was worrying about her business again, and the finances. Gideon didn't want her worrying about anything tonight. Heck, he didn't want her thinking about anything but how good he could make her feel.

To prove it, he put his glass on the ledge of the tub and grabbed a puffy sponge that was there instead.

"Move up here, sit between my legs and let me wash your back," he said, hoping to divert her thoughts.

She did as he asked, settling back against him and sighing more in pleasure than worry as he ran the soap and then the hot water over her skin. It wasn't long before having even the sponge between his hands and her body was too much interference, and he took her glass, setting it with his. Continuing to wash her, front and back, with only his hands erased everything but the moment for him, as well.

What a lovely moment it was, he thought as she rested her head back on his shoulder, letting him find her mouth.

If only he could make it last.

6

CALLA WALKED QUICKLY amid a swirl of falling snow. She was exhausted—and exhilarated. Gideon had kept her awake long past her usual bedtime, but it had been worth being tired and running late.

It was past seven. She usually got to work around five in the morning, but she didn't regret it.

No doubt he'd be angry she'd left without waking him, daring to head out into the world alone. It was morning commute time in the city, people everywhere—she had no doubt she'd be perfectly safe. She had left him a note, but let him sleep. There was no need for him to be up this early.

Calla also needed to loosen the connection developing between them. She understood now why Gideon took his responsibility to her brother so seriously, but it couldn't go on forever—his protection or their affair. Christmas was just one day away. She had to work, and Gideon had to head back to Houston. Who knew when the man who'd mugged her would be caught, if ever. She and Gideon both had to get on with life.

Her heart twisted with a pang of some dull emotion at the thought—regret?

Maybe. If they had time, if things were different…if they lived in the same place, if he'd sought her out on his own, not because he felt he owed her brother, then maybe…but none of that was the case.

Gideon, she'd realized last night, was in a vulnerable place in his life. He'd lost his only parent and he'd come to New York in part to escape his grief. Last night there had been a moment, an unbearably intimate second when she'd seen something in his face, in his eyes, that was so much more than desire.

It had scared her, because something inside of her had responded in kind. But it was only a moment, which was all it ever could be.

She grabbed a second cup of coffee at the café down the street from her shop and was surprised to see a few people already gathered outside.

"Oh, is your beau not here?" one older lady asked.

"I beg your pardon?" Calla asked, momentarily confused.

"My friend Mildred was here yesterday and said you had a romance going on in the shop window. I love romance, and so I had to come down and see, but I work in the afternoons. Millie said he was gorgeous and I wanted to get a peek."

Calla was dumbfounded and found herself staring mutely into the dozen or so eager faces waiting for her response.

"I think, um, I... No, he's not here right now."

They looked so disappointed.

"But I'm happy to work so you can see the cake I'm finishing today, and I might have some samples inside I can bring out to go with your coffees," she offered.

"Oh, that would be lovely. Thank you. We've been admiring the pictures in the window. My granddaughter might get engaged for Christmas, and if she does, I'll be sure to tell her about you. Maybe one of your cakes could be my gift to her."

Calla brightened. "That would be lovely. I can make a design appointment at your convenience"

Hurrying inside the bakery, Calla took off her boots and coat and quickly checked her phone to find a number she didn't recognize, and a message. Not Gideon.

It was Detective Howser. Letting her know her assailant had been caught. Relief had her leaning back against the counter, until he asked her if she could come to the station to identify the man. Calla's hands turned cold, and she put the phone back in her bag. She could identify the man, and she would, but it made her nervous all the same.

She remembered the people waiting outside and switched gears. Opening the shades and flipping the sign, she turned on the lights and grabbed her remaining samples from the refrigerator. There seemed to be even more people outside waiting now, she noticed with a glance.

She was met with some pleased comments and light applause as she walked out. She smiled and then found herself looking up into Gideon's tense face.

"Why didn't you wake me? You shouldn't be out alone when—"

"Good morning to you, too," she said, sending him a pointed look before she passed out her samples.

"Oh, he *is* handsome," Millie said. "If you're lucky, maybe you'll be making your own wedding cake before long."

Calla forced a smile and realized the applause she heard must have been for Gideon's arrival—not for her cake.

Whatever.

She emptied the tray and went back inside, her nerves frayed. The audience outside her window didn't want to see her work. They wanted a show—a romance, of all things. She didn't need this right now.

She heard the door close and Gideon's heavy step cross the floor behind her. She was also intently aware of the onlookers peering inside, and she had to fight the urge to close the shades again. Grabbing a cake from the refrigerator, along with frosting, she started preparing her workspace.

"Calla—"

"They found him."

The short statement stopped him in his tracks, and she took the moment of pause to study him. He was the handsomest man she'd ever known. It was true eight years ago, and it was still true. Even more so—life had weathered him in exactly the right ways, roughening his expression, adding gravel to his voice, depth to his eyes. Neither one of them moved.

"What?"

"I got a call from the detective. They have the thief in custody, or at least they think they do. I need to go ID him."

Gideon was quiet, pushing his hands through his crisp, dark hair as he took in what she was saying.

The crowd outside the window seemed to have doubled, she noticed, sliding a glance that way. Momentarily she thought about taking him back to her office where they could talk privately, but who knew what they'd think if she did that.

She smiled and fussed with the cake and her tools as she talked, trying to appear casual and busy.

"So, you know, there's no reason I couldn't be out on my own this morning," she said a bit too brightly, turning away. She left out that she hadn't known her attacker had been caught until she got to the shop. "And there's really no more reason for you to hang out here now. I'm fine."

Gideon's head snapped up as his eyes narrowed, making her heart leap. He looked angry instead of relieved, pinning her with a look that held her in her tracks.

"What?" Her tone was defiant. Kind of.

"There's no reason for me to be here? I'd say last night gives me some reason."

Calla crossed her arms and rubbed her hands over her elbows. "Well, I mean, you stayed because you thought I was in some danger, but now I'm not. So if you want to go, you know, there's nothing keeping you."

Before she could say another word, he closed the space between them. His body brushed hers, enough to make her want to press forward and complete the contact, but she didn't.

"Gideon, everyone is watching," she said softly, trying to slide away.

He didn't let her. "I don't care."

"Well, I do! This is my business. My life. People used to come here to watch me work. Now they want to come here to see you, and…us. And there is no us! What happens when they find out I'm a fraud?"

His gaze moved to her lips before returning to her eyes.

"Are you saying none of this, nothing between us, was real?"

"No. I mean, it's not like that."

"Then what is it like? Last night felt pretty darned real to me."

"Last night was…incredible. But we both knew you'd eventually go back, and I need to focus on the shop. It isn't that I don't want more—" She paused. More what? More sex? Or more…*more?* "—but the timing is wrong."

"I see," he said tightly.

"Gideon," she said more softly. Forgetting about their audience, she raised a hand to his face, but he backed away.

It stung to have him move away from her touch. More than she would have expected.

"I'm sorry," she said. "I appreciate everything you've done, all of your help, but I just can't let this—" she glanced at the window, at the rapt faces looking on "—go any further. I need to think about the image of the shop."

"When do you have to go?" he asked.

"What?"

"To the police station."

"I don't know. Later. I'll call and find out."

"I want to be there. I want to know that they got the right guy."

She hesitated, but nodded. "Okay."

Something changed in his features, a glint in his eye making her wonder what thoughts were going on behind that handsome face.

"I'll see you later, Calla," he said softly, turning to the door.

It wasn't a goodbye, not a final one, and she was more relieved than she should be.

Calla watched as he left. He stopped when one of the women watching them put a hand on his arm and appeared to be asking him something. He answered, slinging his arm around her and turning away from Calla. Some others joined them.

Would Gideon bad-mouth her? No. She dismissed the idea immediately.

He would never do that, no matter what. She donned her chef's coat and hat, trying not to watch, but her breath caught as he moved away from the group. Before he disappeared, she caught his eye, her heart stuttering at the slant of his crooked smile.

After that, Calla found it very difficult to focus on her work, indeed.

GIDEON WAS NERVOUS.

He couldn't remember the last time he'd been nervous about a woman, but Calla had him on edge. He'd been ready to walk away at the shop, to let her be, as she requested, but a few women in the crowd had offered some kind advice—and encouragement. It reminded him of advice his mom might have offered, had she been here. She would have liked Calla, he imagined. Similarly, she would have told him not to walk away.

He needed a change. Maybe that was the worst time to jump into a relationship, but he felt reenergized by this city and by Calla, too.

Could he love her? This quickly?

He wanted the chance to find out.

At the moment, he stood in the corner of Detective Howser's office, watching as Calla reviewed suspects on a computer screen. She was calm and collected, but he saw her flinch slightly when they showed the right guy, and she pointed him out.

Gideon felt a rush of relief. At least the jerk would be off the streets now.

"Thank you for your time, Ms. Michaels," Howser said, and winked. "You have a wonderful holiday."

"I will now, Detective. Thank you so much for all you've done. Please let me know if you ever need a cake for a special occasion—you get the friends-and-family discount," she said with a smile.

"I'll keep that in mind," Howser said, taking the card and putting it in his pocket.

Calla looked at Gideon for a second, as if she didn't know quite what to say, and then excused herself. Gideon followed suit, but instead of following her, he went in the other direction.

He had arrangements to make.

Stopping on the snowy sidewalk, he grabbed his cell and dialed.

"Gideon, how's it going?"

"Good, Nate. Calla just ID'd the guy and he's toast. Going away for a while, on this and related charges."

"So she's good?"

"She's…amazing."

Gideon waited a moment, holding his breath.

"I see," Nate responded, and Gideon didn't know what to make of it. "So I guess you're staying longer?"

"Yeah, that's what I was hoping. If she feels the same way."

"You don't know that yet?"

"It's…complicated."

"Well, go uncomplicate it, then. And don't screw it up. That's my sister, so you'd better treat her right," Nathan said, this time with a chuckle that made Gideon relax. "And Merry Christmas."

"You, too, bud. Thanks."

After calling in an order for a bouquet of Christmas roses,

he made his way back toward Chelsea and Calla's Cakes, hoping his plan worked. Calla didn't have time to go out every night, so he was going to bring the date to her and show her that he wasn't giving up.

7

LATER THAT EVENING, Gideon emerged from his hotel room dressed in a suit and wool coat that he'd paid a month's salary for. He had to admit, it felt pretty good. He'd never really thought of himself as a suit guy, but the clothing made him feel ready to take on the city. It even changed how he walked down the street. He hoped it impressed Calla. Under his arm, he carried a large box. A gift for her, too.

As he turned the corner down the street from the store, he saw there was a very large crowd in front, and if he wasn't mistaken, someone with a camera. A video camera. Perfect. He ducked into the florist's, paid for the roses he'd ordered earlier and tucked the large bouquet under his arm.

The catering truck was also parked down the street; he approached them, letting them know it was go time.

Smiling, he walked up to the crowd. Some of them recognized him before he got to the door.

"Oh, there he is!"

"Don't give up, Gideon. You two belong together!"

He had to admit it felt odd facing strangers who had such an interest in his love life, but he smiled at them conspiratorially.

"Is everyone ready?"

"Just say when," a man at the front responded.

Gideon looked up to see Calla staring at him, as if wondering what he was doing. Her eyes took in his coat and suit, widening as she did so.

She'd finished the bell cake, which was what he'd hoped. He knew she had to get it to the restaurant in the morning.

"Wish me luck," he said to the crowd, and went inside.

"Hi, Calla," he said, surprised at how nervous he sounded. Clearing his throat, he tried again. "These are for you."

She looked surprised and absolutely gorgeous. And tired. And incredibly sexy.

"Oh, they're beautiful, thank you. What are they for?"

"They're for you."

"Gideon, I—"

He didn't let her object, but tugged her forward and planted a kiss on her lips before she could. It had only been hours, but he missed her. Missed her touch, her voice and her kisses.

Applause from the sidewalk had him backing away, keeping the kiss chaste. He had a mission, and this was only the first step.

Calla's cheeks were flushed, her lips rosy.

"What's with the suit?"

"You'll see. Why don't you let me help you take the cake back and clean things up here? Then maybe we can get some dinner."

She looked as though she might object, but then nodded. "That would be nice. It's been a long day."

He helped her lift the cake onto the cart, but not before presenting it and her to the waiting crowd, prompting their applause.

"This cake is perfection, Calla. What you do is so special. I hope you realize that."

She bit her lip, looking a little misty, and didn't say anything. They rolled the cake back and into the large refrigerator unit, closing it in securely for the night.

Calla didn't look at him for a moment, her hand planted on the refrigerator door.

"Are you okay?"

She nodded, then turned to look at him, her eyes sad. "I'm sorry, Gideon, for being so harsh earlier. I didn't mean to be, and I never want to hurt you. You've been wonderful, but I—"

"I know. It's okay," he said, unbuttoning her chef's jacket for her and releasing her hair from its confines under the hat she wore.

When the long silky tresses fell around her face, he couldn't resist the moment and slipped his hand into them, pulling her forward for a kiss.

She melted under him as if she'd been as hungry for the contact as he was, and that made it very hard to pull away. He heard the front door shut, and, figuring things were set up, pulled away. There was a lot more left to this evening.

"I'll have to go home and change if where we're going requires a suit like that. It's gorgeous," she said, running her hand over the lapel.

"You're perfect as you are, but here, this is for you," he said, reaching for the gift box he'd put down by the entry to the back.

"You bought me a gift? But it's not even Christmas for one more day."

"Just open it and put it on, if you like it. I'll meet you out front."

He left her without another word. After ten minutes, he considered going back after her. Then she walked out of the back room. His jaw dropped as he took in the sheath of red that wrapped around her body, accenting every beautiful inch of her. Her hair was still down, loose, and she kept looking down at the dress as if she couldn't believe it, either.

"You are so beautiful," he managed, his throat tight.

"The shoes are perfect," she said, bending a knee as she looked down at the sparkling silver heel that the clerk had convinced him would be perfect with the dress. "How did you know what size?"

"I know what your foot feels like in my hand, what size it was…I guessed from there."

"I don't know what to say," she said, as she saw the white worktable where she usually sat transformed by a lace tablecloth, china, silver, candles and the roses. A cart with silver trays of prepared foods waited for them. The lights in the shop had dimmed, making it softer and more romantic.

Calla's hand went to her mouth, lips parted in shock, her eyes wide.

"Gideon, did you do all of this?"

"It was a group effort, you might say." He smiled and led her to the table.

She sat as he turned to the people on the sidewalk and nodded.

One by one, they lifted candles and started singing "Joy to the World."

Calla smiled and let out a surprised laugh, applauding them as they finished and then started a new tune.

"I can't believe you did all of this."

"I wanted to let you know how special you are. And they think so, too."

Gideon uncovered a feast of goodies, and Calla's eyes widened as she saw several of her favorites, some delicacies made by chefs she knew in the city.

"How…?"

"I asked Diego for some help. He put me in touch with the right people, and the caterer took care of the rest."

When she saw the bottle of wine he presented, her heart slammed in her chest. It cost a fortune.

"Gideon, this is too much."

Was it because it was goodbye? A final romantic gesture?

Calla found her eyes stinging at the prospect. But what other choice was there? They could try something long-distance, but with his work and hers, it was unlikely they could make it happen.

He took his seat, though he seemed more focused on her than the food. Lifting his glass, he simply said, "Merry Christmas, Calla."

She lifted hers with a slightly shaking hand. "Merry Christmas, Gideon. This is lovely. Thank you."

No one had ever done anything so extravagant for her, and Calla could hardly take it in as they ate. The carolers sang several more songs and then moved on down the street, entertaining passersby. After they finished their dinner, Gideon pulled his phone from his pocket and popped it into a docking device on the counter; pretty strains of holiday guitar music filled the space.

He held his hand out to her, and she took it, letting him pull her up close.

Dancing. She was *dancing* in her store. With Gideon.

It was like some kind of dream. The wonderful kind.

Except that she was about to wake up, without him, when he left.

As he tipped her face up for a kiss, she realized in sudden panic that she didn't want that. But what else could he do?

"What's wrong?" he asked, clearly sensing her tension. He frowned as he looked down into her eyes.

"I—I... This is so wonderful. You're so wonderful. I know I have no right to ask, and that I said this was a temporary thing, but—"

He stilled, too, a strange expression on his face. Calla choked, unsure. She was being needy and clingy, which she hated, but he was leaving anyway, so what did she have to lose?

"Calla? What is it?"

She took a deep breath.

"I don't want you to go. I mean, I know you have to, you can't just stay here, you have a life back in Houston, but…if you wanted… If you were interested…in more…" She took a nervous breath. "Maybe we could work something out. Visit, talk online, maybe. I could try to get away, to come to see you…or something."

"Oh, Calla," he said on a sigh, chuckling and pulling her deep into a hug.

Calla wrapped her arms around him, too, but she wasn't sure what *Oh, Calla* meant.

Oh, Calla, don't be silly?

Oh, Calla, stop dreaming?

Oh, Calla, I want that, too?

Wait.

"What did you say?" she asked, pulling back a little to look up into his face.

"I want that, too."

"You do?"

She'd thought she'd imagined it.

"I do."

"Just for the holiday," she offered hopefully. "I mean, if you could take off a little more time from work, and you could stay with me, instead of at the hotel, to save some of the cost."

He ran his fingers through her hair in that way he did, making her lose track of everything for a moment.

"That would be nice. Would you mind if I stayed longer?"

"How long?"

"Until I got a place of my own?"

Was her mind playing tricks again?

"A place of your own? Here?"

"That's the point, right? I want to be with you, to give this a shot…and since I'm pretty sure I'm more than half in love with you already, I don't think occasional visits are going to suffice."

No one had ever made the word *suffice* sound so earthy, so sexy that it ran along her skin like a silk ribbon—but maybe that was because he'd said it as his lips were brushing over her ear.

Her brain caught up with the rest a few seconds later.

"You…love me?"

"Pretty sure."

Those wonderful lips were on her neck now.

"What do you need to be absolutely sure?"

"As much time and opportunity as you'll give me."

"Oh. I think that makes sense. I'm more than half in love with you, too, and more time to…oh…explore that sounds good."

"We definitely need to explore the idea, in great detail."

"What about your job?" she asked more seriously, fighting for clarity.

This was a fantasy moment, but reality waited at the edge.

"I already talked about that with Nathan. I think he'd rather I stay here, too. Keep an eye on his sister."

Calla's eyes widened. "He said that?"

"He more or less ordered me to do it, and you know I can't let my partner down."

Happiness welled in Calla's heart. Suddenly, the uncertainty that had plagued her was replaced with a suffusing sense of everything being okay. Everything was going to be okay. She was sure of it.

"Well, the city is a dangerous place. It would be nice to have someone watching my back," she said as she ran her hands over his.

"I can do that," he murmured, his fingers playing with the zipper at the back of her dress.

"Hold that thought," she said with a grin, pulling away and walking to the windows, waving to the people passing by and the few who'd stopped to watch as she closed the shades, one by one, until they were alone.

Returning to his arms, she looked up into the face of the man she was going to spend the holiday with, and every day after.

"Now, where were we?"

He remembered perfectly, his lips finding hers, his fingers going back to the dress with more purpose, and Calla smiled into his kiss, thinking it was absolutely going to be the best Christmas ever.

* * * * *

PLAYING GAMES

Meg Maguire

For my husband—copilot for all my best road trips, bedmate in sketchy, spiderful honeymoon suites.

1

CARRIE LEANED TO one side, stealing a glance at the line's progression—or lack thereof. Seemed as if it hadn't moved in ten minutes or more.

One of the clerks behind the rental car counter boomed, "Again, any customers with reservations, please move to the right-hand line. Everyone else, please stay to the left, and we'll do our best to accommodate you."

Carrie willed her heart to slow, but it was looking grim. Her Sacramento–Portland flight wasn't the only one to get canceled. The unusual ice-and-wind storm that had hit western Oregon was laughable by Midwest standards, but it was more than enough to grind the under-prepared region to a halt. Everyone in this line had the same idea—screw waiting for the next available flight north. That could take a day or more. Instead, rent a car and drive an all-nighter, whatever it took to get home for Christmas morning.

There were businessmen in the queue, ones who probably had kids looking forward to their arrival as much as they did any gift from Santa. There were families, too, like the young mom a couple spots ahead of Carrie, with a toddler flopped unconscious on her chest, chubby cheek on her shoulder. There was Carrie, who didn't have kids to see, but whose younger brother, Shawn, was due to pull into the Grafton Amtrak station the following lunchtime. She wasn't going to miss greeting him for the world, waving from the platform beside their mom and dad. She hadn't seen Shawn in over two years. Not since she'd hugged him goodbye before he'd shipped out for his second tour in Afghanistan. Normally, sure, she'd defer to the people with kids to get home to. But she needed this car as badly as any of them.

One person who *didn't* need a car so badly, she imagined, was the guy in front of her. She hadn't seen his face, but he was probably her age—thirtyish—and he was single or at least childless. She knew because she'd listened to his phone call when she'd gotten in line half an hour earlier. He'd greeted his mother, explained that his flight had been nixed and that he'd call when he had an update. That was that. No, "Tell the kids I'll get there as soon as I can." No follow-up call to the wife. If anything, he'd sounded tired and cranky, his entire aura transmitting that his trip was one-hundred-percent obligatory.

You, Carrie thought, glaring at his neck above his smoky-smelling black hoodie, *should spend the night in the airport if they run out of cars. Let the people who want to get home be on their merry way.*

She studied his short dark hair, trying to find fault with it. No luck. Or with the olive duffel bag slung over his shoulder, but that reminded her of her brother, so no criticism there. With his butt in those jeans... Damn, no issues with that, either.

Finally, the line progressed a space. The mother and co-matose toddler stepped up to the counter, which put Carrie within striking distance right after the grump. Thank *God.* She couldn't stand keeping still. It was a wonder she hadn't been labeled ADHD in grade school. Instead, her mom had diagnosed her with a severe case of ants-in-the-pants and signed her up for peewee athletics. She'd gone to the state championships for track and field her junior and senior years, and had gotten a scholarship for it, too. So, hey, good as medication. What she'd give for a jog bra right now... Though, God knew what the TSA would do with random women caught running laps through the terminal to save their sanity.

"Next," called the clerk, and the grump stepped to the counter.

"Whatever you've got," the man said.

"What we've got is exactly one car," the clerk replied, typing.

Carrie's heart stopped.

"Hope you like subcompacts," the clerk added with a smile, and Carrie surged forward on a wave of desperation.

"Wait! Hi, sorry," she said, half to the clerk and half to the grump. "There's only one car left?"

Murmurs rose behind her from the dozen or more people still trapped in line.

Seeming to steel herself, the clerk told the crowd firmly, "That's correct. There is only one car left. I suggest you all try the Avis counter. They may still have vehicles."

"When is the next car due to be returned?" someone called.

"The Avis counter," repeated the clerk gruffly. "I'm sorry. The cancellations have created a volume we're not equipped to deal with."

This invited more grumbling, but also the scuffing of shoes as many hurried away to try their luck in the other rental car queue. Carrie didn't bother. She had line fatigue. She was punchy. She was righteous, and this guy did *not* deserve the last car.

"Can you check again?" she asked, standing right beside him as if they were a couple. She didn't look at his face, but she could guess he was miffed. "Please," she said. "I *have* to get home by tomorrow morning."

"Don't we all," muttered the clerk, and she swiveled the computer monitor, tapping a little box in the upper corner that read, *Vehicles in reserve: 0*. "I'm sorry, ma'am, but we're all out."

Carrie turned to the grump and was met by hazel eyes—brownish gold—and black stubble. She was zapped by a weird recognition, one she couldn't place. He was freaky handsome, though. Was she bickering with someone famous? Right now, she couldn't manage to care.

"I'll give you a hundred dollars," she told him. "Please. A hundred bucks for that car."

"Ma'am," began the clerk, probably about to point out some bribery law Carrie was trying to violate. But whatever the woman said next went unheard, as the grump's brows drew together and he said, "Carrie?"

"Excuse me?"

"Carrie Baxter."

She blinked. "Yes. Do I know you?"

Something went dark in his eyes at that, and he probably would have frowned if his expression wasn't already thoroughly sour. She studied him, and there was that spark of familiarity again. She definitely hadn't slept with him. She'd remember sleeping with someone this handsome. With those cheekbones and black brows, and intense eyes. Oh, shit. Wait. Those eyes.

A surprised "Daniel" fell from her lips.

Daniel Barber. Oh Lord, her high school boyfriend's best friend. Her line-up mate for much of school until Andrea Batagglia had moved to town their sophomore year and wedged herself between them alphabetically. Jesus, he looked as broody and annoyed as he had as a teenager. And as unapologetic as the day he'd destroyed her relationship.

"Are you going home?" he asked. "To Grafton?"

"Yeah." Oh, hey… "Are you?"

"Yep."

Oh— *hey!* Oh, no. Eight hours in a car with Daniel Barber, probably longer if the roads were icy.

"Two hundred dollars?" she ventured.

"Let's just…carpool." He said it stiffly, his tone suggesting that had there been extra cars, there was no way in hell he'd have made the offer.

And did she have a choice, really? Hours in a car with the grown-up version of the ill-tempered boy who'd intimidated her in high school, scowling every time she interrupted him and her ex when they'd been talking about dude crap. Who'd smiled at her maybe twice in their entire twelve years of overlapping, small-town education. Who'd smoked beneath the bleachers during her track practices, those hazel eyes finding her through the steps and beaming the coldest mix of judgment and ambivalence. He'd played bass in her ex's awful band, too, shooting her dirty looks when she sat in on their practices. Figured. The attitudinally challenged burnout and the overachieving jock girl—different species back then. Back when he'd dismantled her relationship, ostensibly for the sport of it.

But now, more than a dozen years later, they were just strangers. Two thirtysomethings headed in the same direction, both wanting only to get home for Christmas.

"Fine," she said. "That'd be good. We can take turns driving." And sleeping. That way, they'd never have to talk.

Daniel turned back to the clerk and continued the transaction, and Carrie offered her driver's license so she could be covered by the insurance. Just like that, she was bound to the man who'd made her teenage years especially awkward.

Daniel Barber, with the king-size chip on his shoulder. Daniel Barber, who'd never once cast her a glance that wasn't adversarial or at least annoyed.

Daniel Barber, who'd driven a wedge between her and her first love, inspiring Matt to break her heart two days before their senior prom.

He was the scourge of her youth and now the harbinger of awkward road trips.

Though, goddamn, she thought, stealing a final glance at that stern face. The bad boy had blossomed into one stunning grown-ass man.

2

"SERIOUSLY?" DANIEL ASKED, standing before their rental in the near-empty lot.

The car was tiny. And girly. An eggnog-colored Fiat 500. Under any other circumstances, Carrie would have been delighted, but there was a reason it was the last vehicle to get rented. Taking this little gumdrop of a car into an ice storm wasn't the smartest move.

But *smart* was a luxury that neither of them could afford at the moment.

"It's cute," she said in its defense.

"Let's enter the Iditarod with a team of weenie dogs while we're at it."

"Shut up before you hurt its confidence." She grabbed the key from his hand and unlocked the trunk to stow their bags. "I'll drive first. I want to get this thing figured out before the roads turn sketchy."

Daniel seemed fine with this, obediently heading for the passenger side. He moved his seat back and settled in while Carrie familiarized herself with the controls.

"Buckle up," she said, and then the road trip was on. "Here." She handed him her phone. "Open the map thinger and see if you can program Grafton in."

"No." He set it in the cup holder between them.

"Yes," she said, and shot him a look as she pulled the car out of the lot. "I'm not getting lost in the middle of a freak storm because you think you know the way."

"And I'm not spending the next five hundred-plus miles listening to some robot tell us to stay on I-5 North."

"Tell me how to *find* I-5, then, genius."

He pointed to a sign that very conveniently, very annoyingly appeared as the road curved.

She frowned. "Fine. But I get to pick the radio station." And once they'd merged onto the freeway, she scanned for the perkiest, pop-iest one she could find, just to punish him.

"You're way bossier than I remember," Daniel said.

She considered it. Yes, she was acting a touch pushy. Preemptively, because she was poised for him to do the same. To be all brusque and tactless. To be Daniel Barber, basically.

"People change a lot in thirteen years," she told him. And in more ways than simply becoming devastatingly handsome. Not that she even cared.

"Did you go to our ten-year reunion?" he asked.

"I did." And though it had been more than a decade since she'd last seen Daniel, she'd mingled and danced with her heart throbbing in her throat the entire evening, wondering if he'd show. And if she'd still be livid with him. Was she livid with him now? No, not really. It wasn't as if she and Matt had been destined for wedding bells. All they'd probably been destined for was a half-assed attempt at a long-distance romance when college started, then a breakup that would've ruined both of their Christmas breaks. A mercy, in the end, although *so* not Daniel's place to instigate.

"Did Matt go?" he asked.

"Yeah."

"You guys rekindle your little high school romance?" he asked, a snide edge to the question.

Oh, you mean the two-and-a-half-year, most formative relationship of my life? That you ruined, by telling Matt God knows what horrible lie about me? That old thing?

"We did not," she said coolly. "We danced a few times, but he's married now with a toddler. Do you guys not talk anymore?"

"Facebook's not really my thing."

"Are telephones your thing?" she countered. "Because Matt's vocal cords were working just fine."

She heard him hiss a little sigh through his nose. That sound brought back memories. If the man ever released a fragrance, she knew precisely what to name it: Derision by Daniel Barber.

"He seems really happy," she said. "I met his wife and she's very nice. They only live ten miles from his parents."

"She cute?"

"His wife? Yeah, she's pretty."

"Was that weird for you?"

Ugh. Why did he have to be so exactly like himself even after thirteen years? So mean, always angling to make people uncomfortable?

"No, it wasn't. There's nothing weird about a guy I dated marrying somebody else ages after we broke up. No matter how attractive she is."

"Even though he's the one who dumped you?"

She gritted her teeth. "Why do you ask? Are you making notes for yourself on how human emotions work?" God knew he could use them. She glanced to the side to find him smiling to himself in the faint glow of the dash display. Oh, he had emotions all right. All the jerky ones like smugness and scorn and self-satisfaction.

"Are you still angry about whatever it was you found so repugnant about me back then?" she asked. "Whatever it was that inspired you to convince Matt to dump me?"

Could loyalty actually be on his short list of acceptable feelings?

"Just making conversation." Christ, he didn't even bother denying being the catalyst.

She turned up the radio.

AFTER TWO HOURS of uneventful travel, Carrie pulled off the freeway near Red Bluff. "I'll do another hundred miles, but I need a pit stop."

"Suit yourself."

She pulled the car into a gas station. Daniel topped off the tank while Carrie got a coffee and stretched her legs. She watched him through the store's front window, that familiar person standing beside the little car, his attention on the pump's meter. In all the ways that counted, he hadn't seemed to change. Same attitude issues, same callous sense of so-called humor. But the packaging was new. A little taller, a good deal broader. She could make out the planes of his chest beneath the jacket, and he'd filled out in the legs and hips. And butt. He was a man now, but still dragging around the same teenage boy's baggage.

Same eyes, too. She squeezed her own shut, feeling a headache brewing.

And the saddest part was there'd been a time when he'd kept her up nights. When her body had positively hummed with curiosity over his, back when she'd still been with Matt. She'd considered breaking things off over it, thinking herself a monster for being attracted to her sweetheart's best friend. What kind of girl *did* that?

She'd had it all wrong, she knew now. All that attraction had indicated was that she'd been a horny teenager. Carrie hadn't understood the difference between romantic longing and plain old sexual infatuation then. Lust—that's what she'd felt for Daniel. And she'd read too much into it, let it gnaw at her until it had soured into guilt and nearly driven her to break up with Matt, before he'd ultimately beaten her to it.

When she climbed back behind the wheel, she resolved to pinpoint something redeeming about Daniel. She refused to believe she could have lusted so intensely for this guy if she hadn't sensed *something* intrinsically worthy in him.

Once she'd gotten them back on I-5, she turned down the radio and hazarded more small talk.

"Well, I guess neither of us lives in Sacramento, otherwise we'd be making this trip in our own cars. Where's home for you these days?"

"Coalinga."

"Is that near Fresno?"

"More or less. You still in San Francisco?"

How about that? He'd actually returned her conversational serve.

"I am," she said. "Sunset."

Funny, he'd remembered where she'd moved for school. Then again, the number of things she remembered about him was embarrassing. *Like the way his old jacket smelled.* She'd found that gray hoodie tossed over a chair in the kitchen of Matt's parents' house. He and Daniel and the rest of the band had been practicing in the basement. She'd given in to the urge and had brought the jacket's collar to her nose and breathed him in. She'd caught a hint of cigarettes but other things, too. The curious scent of young manhood, kind of like Matt's, but different.

It had made her wonder if he'd taste different than Matt if she kissed him. It had made her wonder a lot of things that had left her feeling guilty. That curiosity had put her on the road to realizing that, counter to what the fairy tales and romantic movies suggested, loving one person didn't stop you from craving another.

Of course she'd wondered what her attraction to Daniel had meant. Had it meant she didn't love Matt? Or had the fact that Matt hadn't been able to hold her attention been proof that something about her love had been faulty or selfish? He'd been so much *nicer* than Daniel, after all. So much more lovable.

"What kind of degree did you end up earning?" Daniel asked after a couple minutes of silence.

"Business."

"You put it to much use?" he asked. She couldn't tell if he was being snarky again, though no doubt he held business-people in contempt. He was probably a clerk at the country's last surviving record store. Or a professional heckler, something that played to his primary talent—douchiness.

"I manage a climbing gym," Carrie told him.

"Come again?"

"You know, those places where you can do indoor rock climbing. Best in the Bay Area," she chirped, mimicking the TV ads. "With a sixty-five-foot roof and over seventy routes for all skill levels!"

"Weird."

"Yeah, a bit. But it pays pretty well and they let me try new things. It's a good chance to make contacts, too, since I'd like to start my own business someday. Plus, now I've got really good arms, and there's always lots of shirtless men hanging around. As it were."

He didn't even sniff that bait.

The chatter was flagging, so she asked, "Do you still play bass?"

"Nah."

"That's a shame. You were the only half-decent one in the band."

"*Half-decent* hardly equals an artistic calling. I only ever really did that as an excuse to hang out at Matt's, anyway."

She pondered that. She'd always suspected his home life had been less than idyllic. Those suspicions had become starker as she'd grown up, met new friends with dysfunctional families and had come to realize exactly how awful some childhoods could be. Toward the end of high school Daniel had lived with his grandma, which had seemed like a red flag. Maybe she'd find the nerve to pry in the next however many hours of driving.

The conversation lagged for a long time. Carrie caught

herself squinting, her contacts growing sticky and her eyes strained. "I hate night-driving."

"I'll take over."

"That might be smart." The closer they drew to the Oregon border, the gustier it got. "I'll keep going till we're near Shasta."

They made the switch a half hour later, and just in time. Carrie's headache was intensifying, the caffeine leaving her dried out and dim-witted. She sighed as Daniel merged them back onto the freeway, the end nowhere in sight. "We should both be in Grafton by now. And I should be on my second glass of wine with my mom, staring at the Christmas tree."

Daniel didn't volunteer his own plans, and she tried to guess what they might be. She'd never been inside his parents' place—a dumpy little house on the outskirts of town with a steadily rusting hot rod parked on the side lawn. The kind of place where people stocked twenty-four packs of beer and argued a lot. *Merry Christmas from the Barbers.*

"Did your dad ever fix that car that was always sitting in your yard?"

"No. He never finishes anything."

"Do they still live in that same house, by the pond?" she asked.

"Yeah."

"Is that where you're staying?"

A light drizzle had begun to fall, and Daniel switched on the wipers. "No, at my grandma's house. My mom was supposed to pick me up from Portland and drop me there. I'm sure she's happy the storm's saved her the trip."

"Grandma's house… Now I'm picturing you sipping tea and eating homemade cookies."

"My grandma's not that wholesome, though she does bake good cookies."

"Frosted with sprinkles?"

He shook his head. "Gingerbread."

"Hot toddies?"

After a pause. "I don't drink."

"Oh." Interesting.

"Not for a few years now, anyway."

"Do you have issues with it or…?"

Another curt, "Yeah."

"Like addiction?"

He laughed softly. "No. More like it turns me into an even bigger asshole than I usually am."

"Ah." A corner of Carrie's heart softened to hear him admit he was a jerk. "Well, that's a good reason to abstain. I like what a glass of wine does to me. Gives my brain permission to quit overthinking stuff for a couple hours."

He smiled faintly, eyes on the road. "You were funny drunk."

"Oh, God. I don't drink like that—like I did at those parties."

Amateur hour, for sure. Who knew how dumb she'd looked to sober outsiders. To Daniel. She remembered a party at one of the popular kids' houses, drinking a couple too many tumblers of Sprite and vodka, and Daniel showing up late in the festivities, grudgingly at Matt's insistence. He'd been sober. She'd been drunk. She remembered sitting on the floor, giggling at something or other. Some people had been playing a video game and Daniel had crouched beside her. She couldn't recall what she'd said to him, but more than a decade later she knew his response word for word.

You're super wasted, aren't you? He'd said it with a little smile, a glimmer that she'd taken for true fondness amid the teasing. Not that her judgment could have been trusted. He'd probably been mocking her.

She told him now, "I've graduated to beer and wine—and moderation—since then. You still smoke," she added.

Daniel shook his head.

She laughed. "You think I can't smell you?"

"I quit when I was twenty-two."

"High time you washed your— Shit, look out!" A large delivery truck was fishtailing in the slow lane.

Daniel scanned left and merged, giving the truck room to right itself. "Jesus." He sounded rattled.

"Black ice must be forming already." She put a hand to her pounding heart, checking the side mirror and finding the truck stable again. "Nice maneuvering there, Barber."

After a minute, he asked, "What were you saying about me needing to wash something?"

"Your jacket. You kinda reek."

"It's from my job." His tone had changed, tinged with a little defensiveness. Would wonders never cease?

"Jeez, what do you do? Bouncer?" It was the only job she could think of that involved standing around soaking up people's secondhand smoke.

"I'm on a wildfire crew."

She blinked. "Oh."

"This jacket was stuffed in the same bag as the last shirt I worked in," he said, sniffing his sleeve. "Forgot about it until it was time to head out the door for the airport."

"Wildfire crew," she murmured. "That's very…manly." And very admirable, which didn't quite square.

"It's a job," Daniel said. "Interesting one."

Interesting and *dangerous.* Ah. Putting her finger on it, Carrie had to laugh. "You always did have a death wish. Just like my brother—and he's coming back from Afghanistan tomorrow."

"Shawn's in the service? Damn." Then, after a moment's thought, "I could see that, actually. He was bound for that or pro football."

She smiled, surprised he even remembered her brother's name. "Yeah, whatever gave him permission to put on a uniform and go tearing toward enemy lines. Trust me, I wish he'd made pro. I'd take the concussion risk over the dangers he faces over there any day."

"Sure."

"How do your folks feel about the fire-crew stuff?"

He shrugged. "We don't talk much. They seem fine with it. They're probably impressed I have a job at all."

"What about a girlfriend?" Carrie asked, a lump lodging in her throat. "I don't know how I'd sleep if my boyfriend was out in the middle of that stuff. The news footage is terrifying enough without worrying about someone you know."

"A woman who cares enough to worry about me isn't a problem I'd know much about," Daniel said.

She stared at the swatting wipers, her emotions humming static, caught between two frequencies—sadness and relief. The sadness was novel. Daniel had always been too prickly to inspire sympathy, at least when she'd been younger. The relief was simply alarming. Why on earth should she care if this man was single?

She'd been over him for years—both the lust and the bitterness. And the latter should have ruined the former for good. *Should* have.

He was *still* a prickly jerk.

They lived two hundred miles apart.

She shoved that stuff aside. "How did you get into fire-fighting?" It seemed like such a cooperative job. So not the Daniel Barber she'd known.

"I did some logging out of high school. Then wound up in the park service for a while, but I didn't really have the people skills for that."

"You don't say!"

He shot her a funny look and Carrie laughed. "Sorry. Too easy."

"Anyhow, I dunno quite how it happened. Saw a crew opening listed someplace or other, and it sounded exciting. Pays good."

"And is it exciting?"

He nodded. "I'll do it till I'm dead."

The way he said that gave her a shiver. That was where his recklessness and her brother's adrenaline addiction varied. Daniel really did have a death wish, she thought. Or, at the very least, a lack of concern for his own safety. He'd always been the kid who'd climb forty feet up a tree and turn a sixth-grade field trip into a scene. Always diving off the trestle or driving too fast or picking fights with grown men for the sport of it.

"From chopping trees into timber to trying to keep them from burning up," she mused.

"That's me."

Was it? They'd known each other since kindergarten. How come Carrie didn't feel as if she understood this man at all?

"You're a weird guy, Daniel."

"Don't remember asking your opinion."

"Don't remember you ever caring what anybody thought of you." Least of all Carrie. His best friend's annoying girlfriend, that was all she'd ever been to him. Some grade-grubbing jock girl loitering in the basement during their band practices, probably wrecking the bro vibe.

"You don't get into as many fights as I did if you don't give a shit what people think," Daniel said absently.

She frowned, mulling that over. "That's probably true. I guess maybe I always figured you just *liked* fighting."

"Surprised you thought about me at all."

She spoke carefully. "You were Matt's best friend. And it wasn't exactly lost on me that I never had your endorsement."

"You got that part wrong," Daniel said. "You and Matt were perfect for each other."

She sensed something mean coming, some jab that proclaimed both her and Matt equally boring or upstanding or overachieving.

"Go on," she said. "Go ahead and qualify that statement."

"Qualify it? It's true. You guys deserved each other."

"And...?" She twirled her hand. "Because I know for a fact Matt dumped me because you told him to."

"And nothing," he said, shrugging. "He was a good guy. You were a nice girl. And I never told him to dump you."

"Well, you told him something. He said so. He said you guys had a long talk and he realized he had to end things. So forgive me if I assumed you were going to say something mean just now."

"Give me long enough, I probably will."

She sighed, headache reasserting itself. "Four hundred miles to go."

3

DANIEL EYED THE intensifying rain with worry. Rain for now, but the farther north they went, the colder it'd get. This water would be ice and snow before long, and he didn't have a ton of faith in their little wind-up rental.

The highway was quiet, and small wonder. Only the desperate and dumb were out driving in this. The smart people were comfortable indoors sipping eggnog with their loved ones, or whatever it was nice people did for the holidays. Like he'd know. He hadn't celebrated Christmas in six years, probably.

If it was only him along for this ride, he'd have downed a few Red Bulls and powered through the trip, getting there as quickly as possible. But sliding sideways off the road and trapping Carrie with him all night…. The drive was punishment enough for her, surely.

He didn't even want to be making this trip. He wouldn't be if his grandma hadn't called him directly and demanded he come.

This is probably my last Christmas, she'd told him. She was eighty-two and she wasn't a dramatic woman. If she thought this was her final winter, he believed her. *And there's only one thing I'm asking for—everybody to get along for one lousy day. Put aside whatever hurt feelings there are for twelve hours. Suck it up and give me a nice Christmas to remember you all by, wherever I'm headed next.*

He hadn't needed to think twice about it. If that was what she wanted, that was what he'd do. He'd hug the parents he couldn't care less about, swallow his resentment, ignore whatever bait came his way once his dad got toasted, stay away from alcohol himself and keep his cool. For his grandma. He owed her. And he loved her, which he couldn't say about anyone else in the world. Who knew what would've become of him if she hadn't taken him in for his last two years of high school. Probably would've flipped his shit and wound up in juvie or jail if he'd been forced to stay at home.

So, yeah. Whatever Grandma wanted, Grandma would get.

He eyed Carrie, wondering how many people *she* loved. Probably a hundred. And probably they all loved her right back. He didn't even envy whatever happy, homey Christmas she had waiting for her in Grafton. Like he'd even know how to enjoy all that niceness and love and crap. He was allergic to sincerity.

He remembered watching a documentary about the real-life Horse Whisperer and getting that suffocating feeling in his chest. Whatever that emotion was, he didn't even know. He hated feeling touched by things; always felt as if he was choking on something. He avoided interacting with puppies and ducklings and babies. Adorable things made him feel vulnerable, like if he held a baby, it would sense the rottenness in him and start crying, and probably need therapy for the rest of its life. Any time a coworker forwarded an email about a firefighter rescuing an animal, Daniel immediately deleted it. Couldn't risk the sensation. Like a sucker punch to the heart.

The last time he'd cried had been four years ago when one of his colleagues had died in a wildfire outside Yosemite. The reaction had freaked him out so much that he'd had a panic attack and had been rushed to the hospital for shock.

Never again.

Though, God help him when his grandma really did pass away.

In the passenger seat, Carrie was leaning against the window, using a folded sweater as a pillow. He wondered if she was asleep.

He wondered if she still snored.

He wondered if she still used the same shampoo she had in high school, the one that had made her hair smell like strawberries.

Daniel jumped when she spoke, breaking over an hour of perfect peace. "It's after midnight."

"Yeah."

"Merry Christmas, Daniel."

"Oh, right. You, too."

"You can change the station if you want."

He'd forgotten it was even on. The ads and pop music had faded into the droning swish of the wipers. He switched it off.

"It's really coming down." Carrie sat up straight, balling her sweater in her lap. She was right. The drops had turned to slushy flakes. This wouldn't end well. Western Oregon was useless with snow and ice, unequipped to handle either. Three or four inches of snow could shut down a whole county for days.

"If it gets too shady to risk, we'll find a motel," he offered. Hopefully there'd be vacancies, with most people already at their destinations.

"Or a manger," Carrie joked. "In case my virgin birth kicks off early." She rubbed the sweater bulge in her lap.

Daniel smirked at that, then stifled a stupid little pang of jealousy. He knew beyond the shadow of a doubt that she wasn't a virgin. He'd gone camping with her, Matt and another friend once, and had suffered through noises evidencing that fact. He didn't *care* if she was a virgin, her or any other woman. Didn't care what intimate things his best friend had been privy to about Carrie Baxter, not the feel of her body, the smell or taste of her excitement, or the words she'd whispered in the dark tent. Totally. Did not. Care. At all.

Christ, you're such a creep.

IN TIME, THE late hour began to assert itself. Daniel would have berated himself for not napping while Carrie had been driving, but there was no chance he would have succeeded, anyhow. Too shell-shocked, finding himself in this situation—closed in this tiny car with the girl it had taken him so long to get over. It had been three years after graduation before he'd quit thinking about her. Quit dreaming about her. Quit conjuring up her face in less polite moments—which had taken a concerted, cold-turkey effort. Three years, even though he'd never even kissed her, never even held her hand. So, yeah, sleep wouldn't be coming tonight.

"Oregon welcomes you," Carrie murmured as they crossed the border. They'd been climbing steadily for a while when the sign appeared on the right, the wind peaking as they neared the summit of Siskiyou.

"Check your fancy phone." Daniel nodded to where it still sat in the cup holder. "See what the weather's doing in the Rogue Valley." Not that knowing would change a thing. There was pretty much one civilized route to take.

"Yikes," she said. "Only one bar."

He stole glances at Carrie's face, lit up by her phone as she typed. She still had amazing skin. Her hair was shorter, with layers and stuff, but she hadn't gone California blonde or anything. She wore it long enough to put in a ponytail; running still shaped her aesthetic, he'd bet.

He'd smoked under the bleachers and watched her at practice, and he'd thought she looked like somebody who'd run right out of their stupid hometown, ponytail swinging as she'd book it to someplace better. He'd always liked that about her, how she'd been pretty enough to be one of the popular girls, only she always wrecked it—no makeup ever, no qualms about being seen all flushed and sweaty in her track clothes, brown hair frizzy from practice and curling at her temples.

"It's thirty-two in Ashland," she said. "Freezing rain but not crazy heavy."

"What about Grants Pass?"

She tapped and waited. "Thirty-four. Heavy rain."

That could get nasty if the temperature dropped much more. And this car was about as surefooted as a hockey puck.

"If it gets worse we really might want to stop until the morning. Until it's light out and the road crews have a chance to do their inadequate best."

Carrie looked alarmed.

"What?" Daniel asked.

She sank back in her seat. "Nothing. You're right. We can't be stupid about it. I just really, *really* didn't want to miss meeting Shawn at the train station."

"Oh, right."

Man, what did it feel like, missing someone? Daniel loved his grandmother, but he wasn't sure if he missed her. She was so woven into the mess of his childhood and adolescence that it was hard to crave a reunion. Plus, a reunion meant going back to Grafton, a place that held very few nice memories and a ton of bad ones. Why didn't he miss Matt? His best friend, whose house Daniel had escaped to who knew how many times, with whom he'd shared a band, as crappy as they'd been. He didn't really *like* the sensation of being known, though. Anyone who'd ever known Daniel well—Matt, his grandma, that one nice guidance counselor—knew he had feelings, and knew what had made him put up walls and push people away. Anyone who knew you also knew how to hurt you.

Daniel hadn't missed Carrie, either. For those few years after graduation, before he'd managed to forget about her, he'd *craved* her, badly. But that was different.

Beside him, she fidgeted, shifting her legs around.

"You okay?"

"Just achy. This always happens during long car trips."

"You never could sit still."

She smiled, he thought. He sensed it in his periphery as he might feel a warm breeze.

"You—" He gasped, control of the car gone in a breath.

Carrie yelped, gripping her seat as they slid at thirty miles an hour straight across the shoulder and along the guardrail. The front passenger side was screaming, metal-on-metal, sparks flashing. With a hammering heart, Daniel pumped the brakes until the car finally came to a stop.

"Oh, God," Carrie said. Beyond the sturdy rail was the black of a drop-off. A deep ditch, not a cliff, but the way Daniel's body was pulsing, it could have been the Grand Canyon.

He gulped a massive breath. "Holy shit."

They'd lost a headlight and the side mirror, but the car was still running, and the dash wasn't blowing up with any truly fatal warnings. Tires, brakes, axels—all apparently were intact.

After a minute filled with nothing but the pulse of adrenaline, Carrie said, "Thank goodness we got insurance."

He was too freaked to laugh, and instead let himself collapse against the steering wheel, overcome with horror and relief and guilt. Christ, he could have gotten her killed.

He sat up straight. "Screw this shit. We're stopping someplace." No more bumper bowling with the guardrails. No more driving for a minute longer than they had to.

He aimed them toward Ashland. Even at a crawl the car slipped often, but not as badly as the first time. It was snowing, but as they neared civilization the temperature rose to just above freezing. The road was suddenly glazed in black ice, the little car losing its traction every few hundred yards and stopping Daniel's heart all over again. Carrie probably couldn't tell, since her hands weren't on the wheel as his were. She also couldn't feel how tired he was, how sluggish his reflexes were in the wake of the adrenaline rush and at the end of a long-ass week. Though winter was typically kinder as wildfires went, they still happened. Daniel had helped battle a nasty one in southwest Nevada three days earlier, and he never slept well the week after an intense job. With the hour now approaching 1:00 a.m., he was starting to feel impaired.

He exited at the next ramp. "We'll get up early," he promised. "Once it's light and the roads have some sand on them. Better to be trapped in motel rooms than in a tiny car on the side of the road in the middle of nowhere."

"Fair enough."

"Want to see what your phone says there is for motels around here?"

"Sure."

"Oh, wait. I see one." The familiar logo glowed through the drizzle and fog like a beacon.

"That was easy."

Only it wasn't. No Vacancy, read the neon sign. Daniel pulled into the lot anyway. He parked under the awning, grateful that at least they wouldn't break their necks slipping on the icy asphalt.

"Down one eye and one ear," Carrie said sadly, surveying the car's light and mirror and patting its hood. "Poor thing."

"Better it than us." He headed for the door and the front desk.

"Sorry, we're full up," the woman on duty said with an overdone, patronizing frown. "Lots of travelers got stranded on their way north."

"Are there any other places nearby?" Carrie asked.

"Yeah, two—but the La Quinta's full. We called before sending some other folks over there. Last I knew, there were still a few rooms at the Evergreen. That's about three miles east on this same road."

"Thanks," Carrie said. "We'll try there."

Even after just a five-minute stop, the roads had become worse. They were practically laminated in ice, and no sand trucks were to be seen.

"Jesus," Daniel muttered. "Only thing that could make this road slicker is a Zamboni. This place better have rooms."

"Fingers cross—"

The car slipped dramatically on a diagonal, front tires

seeking the shoulder. Daniel wrestled back control and slowed them to ten miles an hour.

After a seeming eternity, the cheap sign for the Evergreen Motor Inn finally appeared down the road. If there weren't any rooms, driving anyplace else wasn't an option. They might just have to beg to rest in the lobby for a few hours until the road crews could do their thing.

"Vacancy sign's lit," Carrie said hopefully. Once they parked she took her suitcase out of the trunk. Daniel followed suit. He nearly wiped out on the ice as he slammed the trunk, and Carrie almost fell trying to catch him. Somehow or other, they both stayed vertical, then skate-shuffled their way to the motel office.

"Merry Christmas," Carrie called when the clerk looked up from her computer.

"And a Merry Christmas to you both. You two sure are intrepid."

"Please tell me you've got rooms," Carrie said, setting her bag before the desk.

"You're in luck! Exactly one left."

Daniel's eyebrows rose to perfectly mirror Carrie's.

"Okay," Carrie said. "Now please tell me it's got double beds."

A shifty smile. "You two not together?"

They both shook their heads emphatically.

"Sorry, just the one bed. It's a big bed, though," said the clerk. "Honeymoon suite."

Daniel shot Carrie a dry look. Christ almighty, now there was a cosmic joke.

"We'll take it," she said. Only choice they had. Daniel gave the clerk his credit card.

"Honeymoon suite comes with a complimentary bottle of wine," the woman announced.

"I don't drink," Daniel said stiffly, but Carrie grinned.

"More for me."

They were handed a key card and a chilled bottle of white.

"Ooh, Willamette Valley," Carrie read off the label.

"Oh, and this," the clerk said and passed Daniel a coupon for ten dollars off a couple's massage at a spa down the road. He forced a smile for the clerk's sake.

"I can't figure out if this is awkward or hilarious," Carrie said as they made their way gingerly across the slick walkway to the one-story motel's farthest room.

"It's lucky," Daniel said, caught by a rare moment of gratitude. "We get to sleep someplace, which is more than the next person to pull in can say."

"True."

Carrie unlocked their door and they finally left the ice rink behind.

"Jeez, it smells like your jacket in here." She set down her bag. "Clearly people don't take the no-smoking rule seriously."

"Probably distracted by all the consummation. Yikes." Daniel looked around. Pretty big room and, cigarette-stink or not, it was heated and looked passably clean. The bed was gigantic, done up in a tacky peach satin comforter with a couple of heart-shaped pillows to round out the farce. He tossed his duffel bag by the door and pulled the curtains shut. Yellow light from the parking lot slipped through the gaps.

"Oh, my God," Carrie said, the final word gobbled up by laughter. "Come here." She was in the far corner, standing before a large pink hot tub.

"Oh, Jesus. Is it heart-shaped?"

She clapped. "It *is!* And that's not all."

He came to stand by her side, ignoring the little rush he felt as their arms brushed. Perfectly centered in the bottom of the tub was a dead black spider, big as a dime.

"Our marriage isn't going to survive this, is it?" he asked.

Carrie punched his shoulder. That chiding little smack affected him the way a tender kiss might.

He was his teenage self again in a flash. She touched me. On purpose.

"Who puts a hot tub in a carpeted room?" he asked.

"The Evergreen Motor Inn, that's who."

He spent a minute leaning over the edge of the tub and blowing on the spider to make sure it really was dead, and Carrie wandered away.

"If we wake up to find it mysteriously missing," he said, straightening, "this honeymoon will be an official success."

She didn't reply. He turned to find her sitting on the edge of the king-size bed, her phone at her ear.

"Mom? Hi. Sorry to call so late. Bad news—we had to stop for the night. The roads are insane down here.... Near Ashland. We're going to wait until they've put some sand down in the morning....I know, but I'm still frustrated. I really wanted to be there to meet Shawn.... Uh-huh...."

Feeling misplaced, as he always did in the presence of familial affection, Daniel headed to the bathroom and shut the door. He stared at himself in the light of the too-bright bulbs above the mirror. How on earth was this happening? How, after thirteen years, was he suddenly spending the night with Carrie Baxter? And *so* not under any circumstances he might have fantasized about when he'd been sixteen, eighteen, twenty.

Is she single? He hadn't had the balls to ask, even after she'd posed a similar question to him. His stubborn, defensive self wasn't programmed to admit that he gave a shit—not about anything. *Especially* not about Carrie's personal life, something that he'd never be a part of.

He wet a washcloth with cold water and scrubbed his face. The lighting made him look about eighty. Not that he cared how he looked.

Goddamn it, he did care, though. Cared more than he had since this woman had last been a part of his daily life, whether she'd realized it or not. Now he had to share a bed with her.

It didn't matter that they'd likely keep on all their clothes. It would still haunt him deeper and longer than any sex he'd ever had. No doubt about that.

Daniel was broken when it came to sex. He'd never once felt close to any of the women he'd taken to bed. He'd felt grateful maybe, and excited of course. But he'd never felt anything that had made him understand why people seemed to think it was a special, joyous thing to do with another human being. He was okay at the actual mechanics of it, he suspected, but he always felt unbearably awkward the second the sweat cooled, leaving two strangers lying on a rumpled bed surrounded by that sex smell. It was only by the insanity of biology that he got laid, really. If it had been up to his brain, he'd deem it more uncomfortable than it was worth.

And what a wonder you're single.

He left the bathroom, and found Carrie filling a plastic cup with wine.

"Sure you don't want any?" she asked.

"Very." He sat on the rim of the hot tub.

"Your loss. It's screw cap." She took a sip. "Oh, it's nice, actually."

"That coupon the desk lady gave me was for a couple's massage," he said.

"Erotic massage, I trust."

Daniel looked dryly around the room, from the satin pillows to the smoke-scented carpet, to the outmoded tube TV, to the pink fiberglass beneath his thighs. "I think this is erotic enough for me already. Best not to chance a heart attack if it gets any hotter."

She smiled at that and drained her cup.

"Slow down there, champ."

"It's been a long day. You're sure you don't—"

"Yes."

Her eyes narrowed. "If you're an alcoholic, you can just tell me. I won't judge you. In fact, I'll dump the rest of this, if—"

"I'm not."

Like he'd told her, alcohol simply turned him into an ass. Of course, he'd really only drunk on his own or in dive bars, and neither setting had been especially cheerful to begin with. In truth, alcohol probably only had done to Daniel what it did to everyone—saturated his emotional armor until it softened enough to let him feel stuff. He didn't like feeling stuff was all. Made him punchy, like strangers were poking at him. Strangers named vulnerability and sadness. And worst of all, loneliness. He remembered Carrie's little slug on his shoulder, and, without meaning to, palmed the spot.

She poured herself another cup, took a sip and then set it on the nightstand. She flopped back on the massive bed, legs dangling over the edge. He studied the shape of her breasts before he caught himself. *No doubt she doesn't want to be here with you.* Especially not if she knew precisely what he'd said to Matt, to cause their breakup. *At least spare her the perving.*

"I'm gonna shower," he said, and stood to shrug out of his jacket. He cast the spider a backward glance, making sure it hadn't moved. "Keep an eye on our mascot."

"Hang on. I need to get these contacts out." She got up and jogged to her bag, then the bathroom, which she vacated a minute later wearing glasses. She flopped back across the covers as Daniel rummaged for his deodorant and toothpaste.

"Toss me the remote," she said.

He did and then shut himself in the bathroom once more. He stripped his clothes, then the paper wrapper from the bar of soap. A small box caught his eye. Sitting beside the lotion and shampoo bottles was a three-pack of complimentary condoms.

"Rub it in, why don't you?"

Carrie's shout came through the thin door. "What was that?"

"Nothing!"

"There better not be spiders in the shower."

"Nope," he called, tugging the curtain wide. "No spiders. Just some asshole you went to high school with."

Her distant laugh made his body warm.

An "Oooh," came from the room. "Hurry. *Gremlins* is on!"

"Get some sleep, you drunkard." He turned on the tap, drowning out whatever retort would have answered him. He kept the water cold and let it scare away the unnerving, giddy feelings that bantering with Carrie had pitching around in his chest. Stupid crush. Couldn't just stay dead like a hot-tub spider.

They could wind up spending eighteen hours together, yet he'd be stuck waiting to forget about her again for another three years, probably.

Goddamn woman.

Goddamn feelings.

Goddamn Christmas and family and guilt and weather.

And goddamn his heart for aching. Figures it'd pick a freak ice storm to finally thaw again, as broken as it was.

4

DURING A COMMERCIAL, Carrie took advantage of Daniel's absence and changed into yoga pants and a long tee. She tried hard to concentrate on the movie, and not imagine what he might look like in the steaming shower, naked.

It was weird, being around him—the subject of her guilty infatuation at age seventeen, eighteen. She would have expected time to neuter the attraction, the way it had her crushes on the celebrities of the day. But Daniel had matured right along with her taste. Subtle changes to his face marked him as a thirty-one-year-old man, not a teenaged boy. Probably had chest hair, too. And rough hands. Maybe some scars from his work—not burns, hopefully, but interesting scrapes, with interesting stories to match. She sipped her wine, blaming her warming body on the alcohol.

The bathroom fan flared as the door opened, and Daniel emerged wearing the same clothes minus his stinky jacket. He looked way too good in jeans. And his arms looked way too nice in that gray T-shirt. And his hair, wet? Forget it.

"Please tell me that's making you tired," he said, nodding to the cup in her hand. "The point of this sleepover is so we're ready to drive again when it gets light out."

"I thought the point of this sleepover was so we wouldn't die on the icy roads."

He frowned. "That, too."

"It's Christmas. Lighten up." Carrie was lounging on what she'd come to think of as her side of the bed, three pillows piled under her head. Daniel eyed her, then went to his duffel and rooted around before disappearing back inside the bathroom. When he came out he'd swapped his jeans for flannel bottoms.

"Oh," she teased, sitting up. "Now it is *officially* a slumber party."

He rolled his eyes at her before tossing his jeans onto his bag and heading for the other side of the bed. She'd stolen most of the pillows, so he sat up against the awful wicker headboard.

"What sleepover games shall we play?" she asked, and sipped her wine. "Truth or Dare?"

"Sure. I dare you to shut up and get some sleep."

"I dare *you* to be nice to me for twenty minutes."

"I lose."

She smiled sadly at that. "What's your problem, anyway?"

He stared at her.

"I never had the guts to ask you that in high school," she said. "But seriously—why were you such a jerk to everyone?"

He shrugged. "I dunno. Maybe some people are just naturally unpleasant."

"Maybe if you had some of this," she said, and leaned over to grab the wine off the nightstand, "you'd discover you have feelings aside from pissed off and judgmental." She refilled her glass.

He reached over and took the bottle, surprising her. He held it in both hands, resting it between his spread legs. Carrie gave herself a hot second to admire those hands before meeting his eyes.

"Want me to dare you?" she offered.

He rolled his eyes, but wonder of wonders, he tilted the bottle to his lips and took a drink.

"Wow, you're surprisingly susceptible to peer pressure."

He made a face as he swallowed, and tried to hand the wine back, but Carrie wouldn't have it. "Hang on to that. Might help you fall asleep."

"So would shutting off the TV and lights."

A tipsy, mischievous corner of Carrie's brain could think of some other things that might put him to sleep. *Bad girl. Worst.*

"Have you played Never Have I Ever?" she asked.

"No."

"Do you know how to play?"

"No. And I don't want—"

"It's easy. Whoever's turn it is makes a statement, like, 'Never have I ever sky-dived.' And if I said that, I wouldn't have to drink, since I've never sky-dived. But if you have, you *do* have to drink. Basically, you try to say something you *haven't* done that you think the other person has, if you want them to get drunk." Before he could protest, she said, "Never have I ever battled a wildfire."

His eyes rolled ceiling-ward.

"Go on. I know you have."

"You realize we're thirty, right?"

"Thirty-one. But we're also trapped together in this weird-ass thirteen-year high school reunion for the night. Let's be eighteen again."

"Thirteen years," Daniel said through a sigh. "Like cicadas."

"Exactly. Every thirteen years I'll sweep into your life like a plague," she threatened grandly. "And I know you've fought a fire, so drink."

"Only to make this game be over quicker." He took a sip.

"Now you," she prompted. "You say something to make me drink."

"You don't seem to need much motivation."

"I was hoping those jeans were your grumpy pants, but clearly your pajamas have the same issue. Just be fun for ten minutes and do the stupid game."

"Fine. I've never—"

"Never have you ever," she corrected.

"I'm meeting you halfway, okay? I've never come first in a track and field meet."

"Only in one event." She took a drink. "Some of the point

of this game is to find out stuff about each other. So we can't just say stuff we already know the other person's done."

He waved a hand to tell her to get on with it already.

"Never have I ever…" Man, what did she want to know about him? "Been in love." And she drank.

Daniel didn't, only held her stare for a long moment. She was about to tell him it was his turn when he slowly brought the bottle to his lips.

Carrie sat up straight. "Oh, ho! Who was she? Who managed to melt that frosty heart of your—"

"I'm playing the game, okay? Can't that be enough?"

She sank back against the pillows. "Fine. Your turn."

He thought. "I've never lived with anyone. As a couple."

She drank. "It lasted, like, six weeks. Okay…never have I ever saved anyone's life."

His gaze ran away at that, darting around the room. The bottle stayed between his legs and his expression went dark.

"Is that a no?"

"Even if it wasn't, that's not something you acknowledge within the context of a drinking game."

Whoa. Daniel Barber had a serious side. Who knew? Then her heart dropped. What if he'd had the opportunity to save someone's life, but had fallen short of the task? Shit. The gravity of his job hadn't fully registered.

"Okay. Sorry. That was too heavy. Let me think of another one…. Oh, I know. Never have I ever had sex outdoors."

The sternness left his expression, nostrils flaring with a silent laugh—a fond remembrance of an extramural fling? She couldn't feel jealous about that. The humanity inherent in it was too exciting. He drank.

"Your turn," she said.

"Drink," he said, nodding to her glass.

"I haven't had sex outside."

"You and Matt when we went camping in the North San-

OFFICIAL OPINION POLL

Dear Reader,

Since you are a book enthusiast, we would like to know what you think.

Inside you will find a short Opinion Poll. Please participate in our poll by sharing your opinion on 3 subjects that are very important to all of us.

To thank you for your participation, we would like to send you **2 FREE BOOKS** and **2 FREE GIFTS!**

Please enjoy them with our compliments.

Sincerely,

Pam Powers

For Your Reading Pleasure...

Get 2 FREE BOOKS from the series you are currently enjoying!

YOUR OPINION POLL
THANK-YOU FREE GIFTS INCLUDE:

▶ **2 FREE BOOKS**
▶ **2 LOVELY SURPRISE GIFTS**

◀ DETACH AND MAIL CARD TODAY! ▼

OFFICIAL OPINION POLL

YOUR OPINION COUNTS!
Please check TRUE or FALSE below to express your opinion about the following statements:

Q1 Do you believe in "true love"?

"TRUE LOVE HAPPENS ONLY ONCE IN A LIFETIME."
○ TRUE
○ FALSE

Q2 Do you think marriage has any value in today's world?
"YOU CAN BE TOTALLY COMMITTED TO SOMEONE WITHOUT BEING MARRIED."
○ TRUE
○ FALSE

Q3 What kind of books do you enjoy?
"A GREAT NOVEL MUST HAVE A HAPPY ENDING."
○ TRUE
○ FALSE

YES! I have placed my sticker in the space provided below. Please send me the **2 FREE books** and **2 FREE gifts** for which I qualify. I understand that I am under no obligation to purchase anything further, as explained on the back of this card.

150/350 HDL GGC9

FIRST NAME

LAST NAME

ADDRESS

APT.#

CITY

STATE/PROV.

ZIP/POSTAL CODE

® and ™ are trademarks owned and used by the trademark owner and/or its licensee.
Printed in the U.S.A.

HB-N14-TF-13

tiam with—what's his name?—Pete Pollard. Junior year spring break."

"What? Matt told you guys?"

"Like he needed to. You two probably scared all the bears away."

She smacked his arm and he laughed, a sound she liked way too much. A sound she wondered if she'd ever heard before.

"Well, that doesn't count anyway," she said. "We were in a tent."

"Drink," he proclaimed, leaning over to top off her dwindling cup.

"Technicality," she grumbled, and took a half sip.

"Shit, I'm already kinda drunk," Daniel said, and then stifled a laugh, if she wasn't mistaken.

"Wow. Cheap date."

"It's been years. I probably have my high school alcohol tolerance back."

"It's adorable. You should drink more often."

He began his turn, probably to change the subject. His cheeks were pink, his eyes bright. "Never have I ever...shit. Um, never have I ever..."

"Just ask a sex question. That's the real point of the game."

"Man, girls are perverted. Uh, never have I ever...done anything with another guy. Or a woman, in your case."

Carrie took a sip, and Daniel's eyes widened. "Long story. Tequila shots. Gay bar. It was just frenching."

"How was it?"

Carrie smiled, making her expression wistful. "She had a crew cut and amazing arms, and a tattoo of a dancing skeleton. And she could kiss, I must admit. Okay, never have I ever...said the wrong name during sex." And she drank.

Daniel stared at her and then began laughing, half-doubled over the bottle.

"Shush. It was really embarrassing."

"With who? And whose name did you say?"

"This guy I dated in college. And I said our RA's name, by mista—"

Daniel just about lost his shit.

She gave him a limp shove. "Shut up. I pled drunkenness."

"Classy. I'm detecting a theme."

"Whatever. You've never done that? Little slip, wrong name pops out?"

He smirked. "Never have I ever been much of a talker in bed."

"Oh, Lord." She took a big slug for that one. "Which apparently you already knew about me."

His smile seemed to soften, and he nodded at her cup. "Your turn."

"Never have I ever met a person I thought I might like to marry. Yet."

Daniel didn't drink. "Never have I ever imagined being a parent."

Carrie took a sip.

"Even though you've never wanted to marry anyone?"

She nodded. "Sure. I'm not saying I want to do it alone, but I'd like to have a kid someday. I can imagine motherhood without picturing the father's face. Or, I can now that I'm over thirty, anyhow. Treacherous ovaries," she grumbled, glaring down at her middle.

"I don't think I could ever imagine that without imagining the marriage, first."

She smiled. "I'm slightly shocked you even believe in marriage."

"Didn't say I did. Hell, I dunno. The wine's working." He took an unsanctioned drink.

"Whose turn is it?" she asked.

"Yours."

She tapped her lips with the rim of the cup. "Never have I ever made a sex tape. That I know about."

Daniel didn't drink. "Never have I ever…had sex with a woman I love."

She frowned, feeling clouded. Feeling confused by that statement, disappointed, sad and strangely relieved. "You said you've been in love, though."

He nodded.

"Oh. Was it unrequited then?"

He drank, seemingly in the affirmative.

She cocked her head. "Was it recent?"

The bottle stayed where it was.

"While ago… Ooh, was it high school?"

He brought the bottle to his lips.

"Oh, wow!"

"Jesus, calm down."

"No way. Okay, let's see… Was it someone in our class?"

Another drink, and the wine was nearly gone.

She dredged her memory for likely girls. Cool, tough ones that fit Daniel. "Was it Michelle Sobiari?"

Nothing.

"Was it one of the burnout girls? Like Amanda Duffy, or that one with the dreadlocks and the ear stretchers?"

More nothing.

"Was it one of the popular girls?"

He hesitated, but didn't drink.

"So not totally *un*popular. Right, who's the exact opposite of you? Oh. Nicole Pelletier? Or the girl who won all the debate things, Jamie something. Or—"

"Jesus Christ, Carrie. Shut *up* already."

She started, taken aback. He'd gone from nearly fun to mean again in a breath, eyes cold. Apparently drinking really did crank his jerk dial to eleven. She shivered.

"Fine. Sorry." Annoyed, she drained her cup and left the bed to toss it in the little trash can next to the bureau. She crouched by the door to unzip her suitcase and dug for her toothbrush and paste.

A word she didn't think she'd ever heard Daniel say drifted softly through the room behind her. "Sorry."

"It's not like you didn't warn me." She shut off the TV on her way to the bathroom. "I'm setting my alarm for six."

"Carrie."

She took a deep breath and then turned to meet his stare. What on earth had she expected? That they'd bond or something? "It's fine. Sorry I upset you. I thought we were having fun…and you're really hard to read."

"I know."

"Let's just get some sleep. You want some water, so you don't wake up totally hung over?"

A pause. "Sure. Please."

She went into the bathroom and peeled the plastic off one of the cups by the taps. She filled it and padded back into the main room, finding Daniel sitting at the end of the bed, hands clasped between his knees. He accepted the cup. "Thanks."

"Sure. My fault if you wake up feeling gross, really."

She was about to step away when his warm, rough fingers circled her wrist. Her heart stopped. Limply, she tried to tug her hand away. "What?"

"I'm not sure if I'm drunk or not," he said, holding her stare. "But I'm going to say I am and blame this on the wine."

"Blame what on—"

"It was you. I was in love with you. In high school."

A deep numbness consumed her body from soles to crown, chased by a hum of rushing chemicals—hormones or adrenaline, she couldn't say which. "You what?"

He let go of her wrist. "You heard me."

"I don't care. Say it again."

"I was in love with you."

"But you hated me. Didn't you?"

"I hated everything *but* you. And Matt," he allowed, breaking their eye contact.

"Whoa."

"Like I said, I'm probably drunk."

"That's...okay. I need to.... Excuse me." She turned, marched to the bathroom and shut herself inside.

5

"Idiot. Idiot, idiot, idiot." Daniel thumped his forehead with the butts of his fists. Rubbed his temples. Stared at his bare feet on the mangy carpet. Christ, if only he could leave. Except stranding Carrie in the middle of the Rogue Valley in an ice storm was definitely more of a jerk move than making her uncomfortable with the world's most awkward love proclamation.

Past tense. He'd told her he'd loved her in high school. And that was true, right? He didn't love her now. Drinking games aside, he didn't know her now. So, how could he—

He froze, watching the bathroom door open and the light inside go dark. He stayed where he sat at the end of the bed, unable to move. She didn't look at him, just walked to her side and tossed one of the hoarded pillows back to his.

"Sorry," he offered, speaking mainly to the hot tub, perhaps the spider. He wasn't brave enough to meet her eyes.

She said nothing at first, stoically folding her glasses and setting them on the nightstand. "That was ages ago... Though, tell me this. Was that why Matt left me? Did you tell him something awful to get him to dump me, thinking I'd run to you instead?"

He huffed a soft laugh. "Yeah. Like you would've ever left him for me."

"What did you say to him, Daniel?"

He swallowed, throat aching. "I told him I thought I was in love with you."

A pause. "And what did he say?"

"I don't want to tell you."

Her smile was dry. "Well, consider it the fine you owe me for making everything awkward."

"At first…we fought. Almost physically. And I told him I knew you'd never want to be with me over him. That I'd only told him because it was eating away at my insides. I felt like, how could I feel all this for my best friend's girlfriend? I'm such a shit. Maybe I wanted him to take a swing at me. I thought, maybe, that'd make going our separate ways after high school easier—him to college, me to whatever. If we ended it on a fight, I could tell myself I didn't care."

"So, why'd he dump me?"

His heart twisted, throat dry and sore, and he spoke to his hands. "He was going to dump you anyway after graduation. That's what he told me after it happened, when I asked if I'd fucked it all up for you guys."

"Oh."

"We had that big blowup, and I guess maybe he felt shitty after, for dragging it out with you. Or maybe guilty, because what I felt for you… It had faded, for him. I don't know. But it sure as hell wasn't to free you up to date me. Neither of us believed for a second you'd ever want that."

She was silent, and he found the nerve to turn and make eye contact. He couldn't read her face, for once. Normally, it was easy. Whatever she felt was written right there. Happy, sad, angry, embarrassed. But the chalkboard was blank.

Whatever she's feeling, it can't be great.

He stood and skirted the bed, and stretched out on his side on top of the covers.

"You'll be cold like that."

He shrugged, shoulders swishing over cheap satin.

Carrie switched off the lamp, and they laid for ten minutes or more in a pathetic charade of sleep. He could hear her breathing as surely as she could hear him. Neither was anywhere close to relaxed. Didn't help that he was all punchy from the sugar, head spinning slightly from the alcohol. Coherent thoughts were about as easy to catch a hold of as gnats.

In barely a whisper, she asked, "Are you awake?"

"Of course I am."

"What are you feeling?"

"I dunno. I never know what I'm feeling. Stupid, maybe. Or creepy. What are you feeling? Pissed?"

"It was thirteen years ago. I don't know that I feel much of anything except surprised. And relieved."

"Oh?"

"I always imagined you must have told him some nasty lie about me or something."

"Never. There's nothing nasty to be said about someone like you."

"That's one man's opinion. But, in all honesty, I think it's kind of sweet."

Daniel sighed. So the last thing he wanted to hear. That his only experience loving a woman was quaint and adorable. Plus it *hadn't* been sweet. Who lusted and ached after their best friend's girlfriend? It had been ugly, made him feel shitty and jealous and wound up and crazy. And, at times, euphoric. The nice-feelings equivalent of the rush he got standing in the path of a wildfire. "Great."

"I had feelings for someone in high school, too."

"Duh."

"Not Matt," she said evenly. "Someone else. While I was with Matt."

"Oh. Wish I'd known that then. Might've wrecked my crush on you."

"It ate me alive, too. I kept waiting for it to go away, but it never did. I felt so guilty about it, that Matt was so great, yet he didn't seem right. Or like, enough. I almost broke up with him, too. You could say he beat me to it."

"Oh?"

"No one had ever told me you could love one guy and still be turned on by other ones."

He turned that around in his head. "Guys get told that sort

of crap, too. About which kinds of girls are just for sex, versus the one magical woman you marry, and who's too good for you to want to do nasty things with."

"Ugh. Why do we feed ourselves that bullshit?"

"I never bought into it. I always thought, why wouldn't I want to marry the woman who makes me feel that the most? Why wouldn't I want to do those nasty things with my wife more than anybody else?"

Carrie laughed softly in the dark. "I'm with you there. I'd be really pissed if I married some guy and found out he used up all the really hot sex with all these skanks who came before me. Maybe *I* want to be his one, most special skank. A skank for keeps."

Daniel snorted. "Yeah. I always thought that was a crock."

"I wish I'd known the whole having-feelings-for-two-people-at-once-is-unforgivable thing was bull back then. I'd have beaten myself up about it a lot less."

"And gotten to be with that guy you liked more than Matt."

"I don't know if I liked him more…. Just differently. He made me feel such different things than Matt did." She laughed. "Matt was the marrying kind."

"Who was your skank, then?"

"Someone I never could have been with."

"Was he dating someone, too?"

"No. He was just off-limits."

"Oh," he said. "Not like…not like a teacher or something?"

"What? Ew."

"Just asking."

"Anyway, I couldn't have been with the other guy. End of story. I was tempted to break up with Matt just so I wouldn't have to feel guilty about it anymore."

"Wish I could have turned off how guilty I felt all the time," Daniel murmured. "From how I felt about you."

"That's so strange."

He frowned, unseen. "I don't think it's strange. Then again,

I couldn't imagine why everyone *wasn't* in love with you. I thought you were amazing." And it was just as amazing that he was even saying these things. Amazing and oddly calming. Freeing.

"I never, *ever* would have guessed," she said. "I was positive you hated me."

"You remember those stupid parties at Jenny Holmes's house, every year when her parents went to the Bahamas?"

"Stupid? I think you mean the awesomest parties of all time."

"Those ones. Where the cool people always wound up in that basement rec room, playing Spin the Bottle."

"And you were always too cool for the so-called cool people," she said. "I don't think I ever once saw you play."

"Like any of the girls would've wanted to kiss me."

"That's not true. Girls can't resist a bad boy."

He smirked. "I didn't wear a leather jacket and have a tattoo, Carrie. I was just an asshole."

"Trust me. You would've been well received."

"I think I was afraid of how you'd react if I played and you got stuck kissing me. Or if your friends would've teased you. Maybe that's why I acted like I thought it was all too stupid to bother with."

"You acted like *everything* was stupid."

He chewed on that. "Yeah, I did. I've never been good at admitting I care about stuff."

"How come?"

"Because if you do, then you have to admit it hurts if you can't have it. Or if it goes away." Goddamn, stupid wine, letting his feelings leak out. He felt a sting in his sinuses and immediately fought to get ahold of himself.

They were silent for a long time, Daniel staring at the stripe of sallow parking lot light painted across the far wall.

Carrie broke the silence. "I wouldn't have given a shit what the other girls thought if I'd kissed you. And if you'd been good at it, I'd have told them so."

He smiled at that. "I always liked that about you. That you could've been one of the popular girls so easily, but even at sixteen, or whatever, you already knew it was bullshit."

"You're giving me way too much credit."

"You could have been the queen of our school. Easy."

"I don't know about that. But if there was any reason I didn't become one of the popular crowd, it wasn't because I thought it was dumb. It probably was because it looked like too much work. You had to look good all the time—makeup and hair, and cute shoes or whatever. Running isn't compatible with any of those things, and I liked running more than I ever wanted people to like me."

"You know, I only smoked for an excuse to stand around under the bleachers and watch you at track practice."

No reply. Shit. Shit, shit, shit. *How much of a stalker could you sound like?*

"Sorry," he added. "That probably came out creepy."

"Nah. Just…surprising."

"You'd have thought it was creepy back then, though. If you'd known."

"You don't know that."

He laughed sadly. "I'm pretty sure you'd have sided with Matt on that. And I'm pretty damn sure he'd have disapproved."

She didn't answer.

"Guess that's enough truth for one night," he said. "We should probably get to sleep."

And he thought he *could* sleep, now. He still felt foolish but also relieved. And it wasn't as if he'd expected this little confession to be received with enthusiasm or for Carrie to echo his feelings. There was no disappointment to suffer. If anything would change, it'd be that this woman wouldn't have to go forward assuming he'd disliked her back then. Not that she'd likely think of him at all in a few weeks…

Ouch.

"'Night, Baxter," he said, and rolled over.

"Good night, Barber."

6

CARRIE DIDN'T THINK she'd ever felt quite what she was feeling now—no longing even half this deep. So deep it hurt. She wanted to turn over, to reach out, to wrap herself around Daniel and feel his body against hers. To kiss him and taste her own desire mirrored in him. To slide her hand low and find him excited—hard from wanting her. Flushed and thrumming, exactly how she felt between her thighs.

Fear held her back. Fear that if she made the leap and bridged the gap, he'd clam up, his muscles being the only part of him growing hard as he locked her out, shut himself down. But she didn't know if fear could hold her back much longer. Fear froze, but desire burned. And everyone knew which would win in a fight between ice and fire.

She'd willed him to press her for the identity of the boy she'd liked as much as Matt, but he hadn't. She didn't know how to make such an announcement now that the conversation had petered out. She only knew what her body wanted to say to him. And she'd always trusted her body above her brain—it was her physical self that kept her mental one in check, after all.

So, after ten minutes of dead silence, she turned things over to instinct.

He was lying on his side facing away from her, on top of the covers. Carrie was beneath them, but she rolled over, edging herself up against his back. He wasn't asleep, or wasn't anymore. He froze as she pressed the fronts of her legs along the backs of his through the tangle of covers. With a guilty thrill, she rested her nose against his warm, hard shoulder and breathed him in.

"Are you awake?" he whispered.

She wrapped her arm around his middle, hand at his ribs and her forearm against his hard belly. "Yeah."

"What are you doing?"

"I'm spooning you. Forwardly."

"Because you're drunk?"

"I don't feel drunk." She felt a lot of things just now, but impaired was *not* among them.

"Is this a pity spooning?"

"It was you," she murmured, and pressed her lips to the collar of his tee. The soft hair at the nape of his neck tickled her nose.

"What was me?"

"You were the boy I wanted so bad that I knew I'd have to break up with…him." She couldn't say the name anymore. He had no place in whatever might come next.

Daniel's body was as rigid as wood. "You're just saying that."

"No, I'm not."

"I know you. You're just saying that so I won't feel like an asshole for telling you what I did."

"I'm nice, Daniel. That's not the same as patronizing. Plus, you're already kind of an asshole."

The tiniest laugh sparked in the dark room, and his muscles softened in her embrace.

"I never let myself really have a crush on you, because I assumed you hated me," she said. "But I wanted you, like I'd never wanted a guy before. More than I probably have since." And for a long time she'd assumed that attraction had been inflated in her memory, some trick of teenage hormones, or blown out of proportion in its one-sidedness, its impropriety, amid all that longing. But lying against him now, smelling his skin, feeling his voice vibrate through both their bodies… "I still feel it. As much as I did then."

A long, reedy exhalation escaped him.

He doesn't believe me. "You used to wear a gray sweatshirt," she said. "Every day, practically."

"Yeah."

"It was a size medium from Old Navy. I know, because once, when you guys were practicing, I smelled it."

He made a funny little noise, a flustered huff warmed by amusement.

"I felt stupid doing it," she went on. "And scared, like someone would come up from the basement and catch me, and *know.* But nobody did. I sort of held it to my nose for a minute. I studied the tag, and how the cuffs were frayed. One of the grommets for the drawstring was missing."

After a long pause, he said, "Your hair used to smell like strawberries. And you wore the same scarf every winter from maybe eighth grade until we graduated. Red and black stripes."

She smiled. "I still have it. It's in my suitcase. Shawn saved up his money and bought it for me. He must have been about eleven. It's from Hot Topic."

His ribs hitched in a little laugh.

"I dragged him in there while our parents were waiting in the RMV for something. I'd forgotten I'd even mentioned wanting that scarf until Christmas morning. He'd never done anything that thoughtful for me before that, not since he'd been really little, anyhow."

"If it makes you feel like any less of a creeper, if I'd been alone in a room with that scarf, I probably would've smelled it," Daniel said.

She splayed her fingers over his heart. It was beating fast beneath taut muscle and the skin she'd never imagined she would ever touch. Boldly, she slipped her palm under the hem of his shirt and up his hard belly and chest. His only response was a silent gasp that swelled his ribs. The heat of him took away her breath. She felt the chest hair he hadn't had back when she'd first lusted for him, and the firm bulk that a physical job had put on his frame.

"Daniel."

He swallowed audibly. "Yeah?"

She slid her palm back down, taking in the planes of his bare body before slipping her hand from under his shirt. "Turn over."

He did. Carrie's vision had adjusted to the ambient light, and she could see emotions in his eyes that she never had before. Vulnerable ones. Uncertainty and wonder. And fire. She did the thing she'd fantasized about so many times, so many years ago, and touched his face. His jaw was stubbly, and it felt good against her palm. As their noses brushed, his eyes closed, but not Carrie's. She watched a furrow gather between his brows, watched his lashes quiver. With a final breath, she pressed her lips to his.

Warm, soft, smooth skin contrasted with his rough chin. She shivered.

His fingers slid through her hair to cup her head, and all at once, his hesitance was gone. His hold was needy and loaded. With a tiny moan, he angled his face and kissed her deeply. It could have been his fingertips between her legs for the way her body reacted. Her desire drew tight in her belly and her arousal demanded more, begged her to wrap her legs around him and feel the evidence of his excitement pressed against her. The blankets were as maddening as a straitjacket.

His tongue stroked hers with a boldness she wouldn't have expected, and through the covers she sensed his hips moving. She let his face go to touch him, memorizing his shapes— the firm swell of his backside, the dip at the side, the hard bone of his hip. The touch only spurred him. His kisses and thrusts intensified, and the fingers in her hair slid down her back under the covers. Carrie eased her hand beneath his pajamas. No shorts. Just her palm on his bare ass. The kiss fell apart. Daniel's lips fled hers to settle against her throat with a groan.

She touched his belly next, thrilled by the taut planes of him, and the sprinkling of hair from his navel to his waistband. His breaths steamed against her skin and he palmed her butt.

As her own hand slid lower, she realized this moment was nothing like the one she'd lived a thousand times over in her teenage fantasies. She'd always imagined her fingertips brushing the cool metal of the buckle and the studs of that old belt Daniel had always worn back then, and the thick denim of his jeans. Not all this soft flannel closed only by a drawstring.

He was stiff already, kicking her pulse into overdrive as she kneaded him through the fabric. He grew harder. Longer. Thicker and heavier until his desire beat against her palm.

"Carrie."

You don't talk during sex, huh? Oh, she'd see about that. She rubbed him until he was panting and she was aching, and the hand on her butt was squeezing in a thoughtless, distracted rhythm.

She plucked the bow of his drawstring free and slipped her fingers under his bottoms, their tips met by soft hair, then hot skin. She was poised to take her time and draw out the teasing for the both of them, when Daniel's hand covered hers, wrapping it around his erection with a curt moan.

She gasped, but Daniel mistook her excitement for alarm. He let go of her. "Sorry."

"Don't be." She gave him a squeeze to prove her hand was right where she wanted it.

"I can get kind of pushy," he murmured. "When I'm…"

"I don't mind. As long as you're not *too* rough." The thought of this cagey man losing control and turning gruff, proving that he had needs and desires… No, she didn't mind at all. "I'd like to see you like that. Passionate."

"That's a nice way to put it."

That was Carrie, always taking a highlighter to the positive. And Daniel was just the opposite, she imagined, underlining whatever disappointments affirmed his surly worldview. Well, she wouldn't be leaving him disappointed tonight. She'd get him so hot all those storm clouds would burn away to nothing.

"There are condoms in the bathroom," Daniel said between harsh breaths. "Should I get them?"

She nodded, releasing him. She kissed his forehead. "Yeah. Get them."

He left the bed, hand cupped to his erection. The shyness of the gesture charmed her. The bathroom lit up, blinding after all that darkness. As Daniel was about to return, she called, "Leave the light on—but close the door partway."

He eased it half-shut behind him, looking at her.

"A little more."

He shut it another inch.

"Perfect." The closest they'd get to mood lighting in this, the world's least romantic honeymoon suite. "Now come to bed."

7

DANIEL'S BLOOD WAS pumping so quickly it was as if he'd never taken a drink. The wine's haze had burned away the second Carrie had rolled over and touched his shoulder. He'd waited too long for any kind of sensual contact with this woman. His body wouldn't stand to dampen it.

As for whether Carrie was still feeling the wine…

What she'd said about his jacket, that couldn't be made up. Only someone who'd suffered from the same infatuation Daniel had could've thought of such a thing. But no one had ever expressed those kinds of feelings to him before. He believed her, but he couldn't begin to absorb it or own it or even trust it.

What his body wanted from hers, though, that was a fact he felt in every cell. He had no choice but to surrender to it.

He set the condom on the nightstand, barely believing what he was looking at. Carrie Baxter, in bed. She was sitting up, hugging her knees and the covers, waiting for him. He took a moment to simply study her.

She smiled. "Yes?"

"Just looking at you. Trying to figure out how this is happening."

"Fate?" she offered. "Christmas miracle?"

"Like a really dirty made-for-TV movie?"

She nodded. "Let's hope so." She moved to her knees, reached for him. He still had one hand cupped over his crotch, and she took his wrist and gently moved it away. Hooking her fingers under his waistband, she drew him closer, and he stepped forward until his knees were touching the mattress. His breath fled as her hand closed around his hidden cock, the pleasure a bolt. The world spun and he put his hand on her shoulder, steadying himself.

With a tug, she exposed him, and that eager hand closed around his pounding erection.

"Carrie."

She touched him as though he mesmerized her. As he'd never been touched before—with patience and wonder. The contact warmed him through. She made him feel soft things, sensations Daniel didn't tend to attract. And maybe for the first time ever, he didn't want to rush past the polite pregame stuff to the sex itself. This felt so good. Not like usual.

Though he knew it made him a jerk, Daniel hated foreplay. It asked of him things he wasn't good at giving—patience and finesse and attentiveness. He knew what he was good at, what he had to offer. It was rough and fast and intense, and usually blessedly impersonal. It wasn't that he disliked the women he hooked up with. It wasn't laziness, not even selfishness…not quite. It was fear of all that soft stuff. Fear of being bad at it. Or incapable of it. Fear of proving himself broken.

But this, he thought, eyes shutting as Carrie's hand stroked and measured. This could go on forever. She made him helpless in a way that liberated him, as if his anxieties simply didn't apply tonight.

The room was hot. The world was hot, the ice storm swallowed in the heat wave. Daniel let go of Carrie's shoulder to peel off his shirt. Her gaze took him in. That, he was used to. There was something that certain women liked about how he looked that apparently trumped his sour personality enough for him to get laid. His job kept him fit, and the way Carrie's eyes moved over him…. Yeah, the risk was worth it on a whole different level, just now.

The pressure was building in him, hot and maddening. He took her hand and moved it away, cool air enclosing his feverish flesh. He flung the covers wide and got to his knees between her legs. She welcomed his body as he lowered himself, her slim thighs wrapping around his hips. He braced himself on his arms, stroked his cock along her sex. His bottoms and her yoga pants were cruel, but the tease felt good. He didn't want to rush tonight. Didn't want to miss a second of this.

"You feel good," she said, stroking him from the shoulders to the wrists.

"You, too. What do you like for…you know, foreplay."

"I like this," she said, thighs squeezing his hips. "And kissing. Touching. Anything. I just want to mess around with you."

Mess around—yes, exactly. The clumsy, excited experimentation that typified teenage sex. He moved, drawing her against him, facing, on their sides. She brought her leg up, hugging it to his hip.

"Wait." He eased her leg away and reached between them to push her stretchy bottoms down. His thumbs found no underwear, and his excitement surged.

She helped him get them all the way off, and Daniel studied her as she stripped away her tee. Between her legs, she was just as he'd always imagined. The girl who'd shunned makeup had grown into a woman who kept things natural. And her bra was simple, just tan cotton. Her sexuality was all in her body—a physical expression, not a trick of packaging. Her body *fascinated* him. It was lean and vital, probably boyish by popular standards, but she'd been shaped by her talents and her passion. Her hands weren't soft. She had calluses, from climbing, he guessed. He loved things like this about her. All that imperfection and humanity and evidence of living. Her personality, perfectly translated to her physical being. He wished he felt so united himself. His body was the doing of his job, his disposition a thing to be endured.

"Here," she whispered. Slender fingers slipped under his waistband, and together they pushed his pants down. Daniel eased her onto her back, ran his hands beneath her to undo her bra clasp. She stripped it away and rolled back onto her side, their naked bodies pressing flush.

"Oh." He had to shut his eyes and just *feel* this. Every

square inch of her naked skin against his. Her small, smooth breasts against his chest, the soft hair between her legs tickling the underside of his cock. Her mouth sought his, and Daniel let his kiss tell her everything he felt for her. He was aching, needy, a little unsure, utterly eager. Things he never expressed through sex—never expressed, period. She brought up her leg and he shifted his hips, his erection pressing along her lips. That changed things, transformed his excitement, making it dark and chaotic and as hot as a jungle. Fiercely biological. It got his hips moving, every instinct demanding he angle his cock and drive it deep. She was wet, their contact a mix of friction and slickness, the latter soon dominating. He moved faster with every breath and every tease of her tongue against his. His hands roamed hungrily over her body.

All at once she wasn't kissing him anymore. Her breaths were heavy and harsh on his jaw, her fingers clutching at his hair, hips frantically mirroring his with every gliding stroke. *Holy shit.*

"You going to come?" he whispered, his palm riding the restless muscles of her lower back.

"Yeah. I am."

"From this?" He made it quicker, their bodies practically quarreling.

"Don't stop."

Not for a billion dollars. Not if the motel was burning to the ground around them.

His heart was pounding, pulse thumping everywhere in his body. Cock throbbing and begging to be quenched.

Then she touched him in a way that transcended sex—stroked him in some pleasurable place suspended between his dick and his brain and his heart. She said, "Daniel."

Her body went stiff, her fingers grasping his hair nearly hard enough to hurt.

He kissed her forehead as she rode her orgasm, urging her hips with his palm. "Good." When she stilled, he slipped hi hand between them, fingertips seeking her clit. She jerked at the contact, then eased. He held still, wanting to feel the pulsations and record the rhythm of her excitement. Wanting so much more. To make it happen again against his fingers or his tongue.

He was good at giving women head, but not for reasons he was proud of. Jerk or not, he believed the woman came first, and oral kept the intimacy contained. As deeply personal as the act was, it felt safe to him. It demanded no eye contact, precluded the dirty talking he found so deeply awkward. And it was a giving act, feeling like it earned him the fast, urgent sex he favored.

But with Carrie, he wanted the contact only. Not the safety. He wanted to know what she tasted like and smelled like, wanted her hands on his head, and her moans and sighs filling the room.

When her breathing slowed, he began to move his fingertips against her softening clit. Her palm had grown hot and damp on his neck, and she squeezed him there.

"You want to…?"

"Not yet," he murmured and kissed her temple. "Lie back."

CARRIE FELT DRUNK on the orgasm. Wine had nothing on infatuation. She did as Daniel urged, her head finding the pillow, her back the rumpled covers. As he moved, she admired all that lean muscle. His body matched the intensity of his face and his personality perfectly. She was excited to watch those muscles really work, braced above her, but no—he moved down on the bed.

Oh.

He got positioned on his elbows and she stroked his hair. "You're full of surprises."

He met her eyes, his face in shadow. "You like this, right?"

She nodded. "I'll miss your voice, though."

"I promise you won't be thinking about that in a minute."

Hcr smile fled the second his tongue glanced her clit. Her short nails raked his scalp and the breath left her in a gasp. She was still sensitized there, though the too-much shock of it was good. Everything with Daniel felt saturated, hyperreal.

He was amazing with his mouth. Every slick, firm stroke wound her tighter. But it wasn't right. Not quite. He felt too far away with Carrie on her back and his face obscured.

"Wait," she whispered, tracing his ear.

He pulled back, looking expectant.

"Would you mind kneeling on the floor? Or is that too—"

It wasn't. He was on the carpet in a breath.

"This side," she said, swinging her legs over the edge. "I want to see you."

He came around to kneel before her. So much better with that handsome face lit dramatically on one side. She didn't lie back, but instead curled in a bit, cupping his head as he brought his talented mouth back to her sex. Her heels rubbed at his shoulder blades as his tongue slid deep, and his hands gripped her hips, rough and possessive. He felt close now that she could hold him this way. He felt like *hers*.

"That's amazing," she murmured.

His lids were shut and she traced his brows, willing his eyes to open. But he seemed lost in concentration. She hoped this felt as wonderful to him as it did to her. Was he tasting the evidence of how badly she wanted him, of how good he'd made her feel?

As the pleasure grew, her hands moved to his neck and shoulders, rubbing, grasping, kneading.

"I want you," she said, eyes shutting. "So much." He could stand right now, sink deep with a single push and let her feel his excitement pulsing, hugged by her own. She tugged at his shoulders. "Daniel."

He paused for only a beat—just long enough to say, "Yeah?"

"I want you." She tugged again. "Now."

"I want to make you come again."

"You will—and you would if you kept going. But I want all of you. Please."

He sat back on his heels, breathing heavily, and met her gaze.

"What?" she asked. His hands were still on her hips, and she stroked the backs of them with her fingertips. The touch seemed to knock his thoughts free.

"I like it kind of…rough."

"Okay. How rough?"

"Nothing crazy…and it's not that I only like it that way. I need that to…you know."

"Sure." Good, yes. Amazing. She'd give anything to see this closed-up man turned frantic and desperate with excitement.

He cleared his throat. "I want to make sure I get you there again first. In case what I need doesn't…work for you."

She smiled. "I'm pretty sure it will. Unless you're leaving something out?"

He shook his head, clearly uncertain.

He didn't trust himself. In exactly what way, she couldn't guess. "You're not going to hurt me or anything," she prompted.

"No, of course not. I mean, not on purpose. I just need it fast. And kind of selfish."

God, please. "If it means you'll be excited, then I guarantee you it'll work for me."

He might have nodded. It was hard to tell, the gesture was so subtle. He took in her sex from where he knelt, his gaze so loaded she swore she could feel it against her swollen lips and clit. Then, out of nowhere, he smiled up at her.

Surprised, she laughed, and squeezed his hands. "What?"

"It's nice down here."

"Oh?"

A sheepish sort of smile. "Being on my knees, for you." Except then he was standing, urging her back on the mattress and climbing on above her, his legs knocking hers wide. "It's nice with you in general." His eyes surveyed her body beneath his, and she returned the admiration. He was still stiff, hovering thick and ready above her belly. She reached between them to clasp him, giving a long, slow pull. He dropped his head with a groan, shoulder blades jutting.

"Better than nice," she said softly and reveled in his reactions for a few more strokes.

His face came up, his look so intense that her hand froze. For a long breath they merely held each other's gazes, Daniel's hazel eyes nearly black in the dim room.

"This is the best thing that's ever happened to me," he said.

Carrie blushed. "It's high up there on my list, too."

He moved her hand from his erection. Dropping down on his forearms, he linked his fingers with hers, holding her hands against the mattress, framing her face. "No," he said. "This is the actual best thing that's ever happened to me. No moment of my life is ever going to be as perfect as this one. Here. With you."

Nothing she could think to say deserved to follow that, so she only regarded him. Memorized those words and his face and this suspended second shared by only the two of them. He swallowed and let go of her hands, sitting up to kneel between her thighs. Grazing her legs, he seemed calm but for the quick breaths flexing his belly. She drew her calves along his sides.

"You know what?" she asked.

"No, what?"

"This really is an awesome honeymoon."

His smile was broad and open, but then his expression darkened as his gaze went to the nightstand and the condom. She remembered what he'd said about needing it rough, and a hot wave of nervous excitement got her blood pumping.

"I'm ready if you are," she said.

"I imagined this for years, but I don't think I could ever be ready for it."

"Too bad for you," she said. "Because it's happening."

Daniel nodded. "Yes. Yes, it is."

8

CARRIE MOVED, GRABBING the condom and then settling against the pillows. Her fingers were clumsy as she opened the wrapper, but she saw that same anticipation mirrored in Daniel. She'd imagined being with him a million times when she'd been younger, but never felt able to guess how he'd be. He'd been so prickly, roughness had usually factored into her hypotheses—even rudeness—but she'd never imagined what sweeter intimacies he might offer. She *never* would have imagined him saying the heartbreaking things he just had.

"Here," she said, tugging him close. His knees were braced wide beneath her legs. She rolled the latex down his length, savoring the moment. Savoring the view—Daniel's strong masculine body looming, backlit and seeming dangerous. He dropped down, planting his palms beside her waist. She held his erection, angling as his hips guided him close. She swept his head along her lips, rocked by a surge of pleasure as it stroked her clit.

"Look at me," he murmured.

She did. Her hand went still, and she let his gaze hold her in thrall as the pressure came. Pressure but no resistance. She was lush and ready, welcoming his slow, measured intrusion. She let go to hold his sides, feeling his muscles flex as he gave her more. Just a tiny pang, a small adjustment of her angle, and when he next slid home he was gliding.

How a man could feel so familiar and so new, she didn't understand. And that was Daniel, essentially. A boy she'd grown up with, yet had never really known, who'd shared her exact secret—an off-limits and confounding infatuation, one neither of them had ever expected would lead to this moment.

"You feel so good," she whispered. To speak any louder might scare reality away.

"So do you." He eased back, slid deep. "Even better than I'd ever guessed."

She reached between them to touch herself, but he stopped her, pinning her hand against the bed. She shivered, the coolness chased by heat to feel that bossy grip on her wrist, that little taste of restraint.

I like it kind of rough.

"Let me," he said. He released her and slipped his hand low, thumb seeking her clit. All his weight was on one arm, the tendons and muscles locked and thrilling.

"I want to see what you like," she said, nudging his hand out of the way. If this was the only night they ever got together, she wanted to know exactly who this man was.

Again, he grabbed her wrist and held her hand down. "What I want," he said slowly, "is to be doing everything."

"Oh." Controlling. "Sure."

He shoved his legs even deeper beneath hers, sharpening the angle. His weight was off his arms now, and he took both of her wrists, pinning them above her head. Not so tight that it alarmed her. Not at all. She was physical. She craved the edgy sensation of her body being challenged, especially like this. His hold was everything dark that she'd tried to project onto him in her bygone fantasies. Rough and pushy but sensual, too. His hips moved with an unexpected grace, strokes smooth and lengthening by the second. He worked his strong body with a sureness she hadn't anticipated.

"You want me to do anything special?" she asked.

"No." He swallowed, eyes closing, hips speeding. "No, I just want to feel like you're mine."

Those words spread fever through her body, and she told him, "I *am* yours."

His eyes opened. For a glorious minute the world was his hands wrapped around her wrists, his muscles pumping, his hard length owning her. Then he let her go. A rough palm cupped her breast as the other slid low. One thumb strummed her clit, the other her nipple. The pleasure met and melded in her belly, urgency sparking.

She reached for him, but he said, "No," the word dark and hard. Exciting. "Keep them above your head."

His cock was surging, the slick motions caressing her lips as that rough thumb circled and rubbed. His racing breaths had become labored moans now, rhythmic and guttural, utterly male. The dynamic he'd set didn't welcome instruction, but if it had, she'd have told him, "Talk to me." She settled instead for these dark sounds, let them stoke her excitement as surely as his hands, or the sight of his laboring muscles.

"I'm close," she panted. She moved the only part of her body she dared, flexing her hips to heighten the penetration. *Talk to me.* "Don't stop. Please."

He controlled her pleasure, and although this wasn't what she'd have given herself—rougher, slower—the fact that he was giving it to her made the mechanics moot. And then he did the thing that trumped any touch. He spoke.

"You gonna come for me?" His eyes were hard and hot, same as that circling thumb.

"Yes."

His hips sped, and Carrie felt the promise of release becoming an inevitability. The pressure he spurred was blazing, tight, almost painful, and she groaned.

"Good. Come on."

And she was there, this orgasm so much more intense than the first, multiplied by his rough voice, his firm touch and his dark eyes burning down at hers. It roared through her, forcing her back off the sheets and making her nails bite into the pillow above her head. As the onslaught eased, Daniel's hips relented. His erection slid slow and luxurious and then stopped all together.

She broke his rule, reaching up to touch his face and neck.

His pulse thumped below his ear, echoed by the stiff heat of him inside of her. He looked disbelieving. And electrified. And beautiful.

"Thank you," she said, her voice thick. She cleared her throat and held his hard arms. She let her hips tell him that his turn had come.

He began to move, building gradually until he was speeding again, pounding hard. His eyes were wild, skin surely flushed.

He groaned. "Turn over. Please."

She made it to her hands and knees—more by his urging than by her own volition. She felt the weight of his hard body pushing into her, his length sliding deep once more. The show was over, Daniel chasing his release with an animal ferocity. His hips hammered and his grip was rough at her waist. One palm slid between her shoulder blades, fingers splaying. She felt held in place, exploited even—and, goddamn, it felt amazing.

She'd been with dominating guys before, and those experiences had run the gamut from exciting to a touch degrading. But with Daniel she felt nothing she had before. She felt a man turned wild from desire. She felt wanted in the most primitive, intoxicating way. She felt high and powerful to have done this to him.

"Oh." His moan was deep and ragged, full of wonder. His hands grew slick against her skin, and those masterful hips were frenetic. She could picture them—picture the entire length of his body in profile, gorgeous and rough.

She reached one arm back, found his fingers with her own. He seemed to rattle apart at the contact, his breathing coming in a string of tight gasps and his motions jerky. The pressure built until she had to steal her hand back, bracing against the impact. Then all at once he went perfectly still.

In that quiet space she listened to his panting breaths and memorized the pulse of his length, held tight inside her. His damp palm slid down her back, and he eased himself out with a breathy groan. Carrie turned onto her back as he collapsed across the covers. He drew his legs in, rubbing his knees.

"All right?" she asked.

"I think I got rug burn. Or sheet burn."

"Poor baby." She flopped her arm against his chest.

"I'll sue the motel for my injuries."

She gasped dramatically and thumped his ribs with her knuckles. "Never. I love this horrible motel. And this horrible room."

His fingertips teased the sensitive skin of her inner forearm. "I'm forgiving them for the spider in light of the free condoms."

"Oh, my God, yes. That alone must be worth a five-star Yelp review."

Once her body had cooled some, Carrie rolled onto her side and tucked her knees against Daniel's hip. "That was awesome."

He nodded, gaze on the ceiling. "Yeah, it was."

"I can't figure out if you're exactly how I'd expected or totally different. Either way, you were exactly how you should be. All gruff and fast and…Daniel Barber-y."

"Not too much, I hope."

"No way."

"That stuff's a preference, really. I don't *always* have to be like that—pushy, I guess. I got smacked around some, when I was a kid." He said it without angst, like it was a flat and faded scar to him now rather than a wound. "I think it's made me kind of…weird. About feeling like I'm having physical stuff directed at me. Stuff I can't predict."

"Oh." Made sense. "You liked when I stroked you, though."

He smiled. "Yeah, I did. Though I wanted like hell to grab your hand and control what you were doing, too."

"I wouldn't have minded that." She kissed his shoulder.

"I like what you had me do, though. I liked kneeling on the

floor for you, and feeling how you held my head. I wouldn't, usually. Usually I'd get annoyed, feeling like somebody was trying to direct me."

"I just wanted to feel connected to you."

He seemed to consider that. "It was nice. Made it feel like…like it excited you, touching me. That you weren't just excited by what I was doing to you."

She stroked his hair and held his gaze. "There's never been anyone I was more thrilled to be with. It could have been the worst sex of my life, and it still would have been amazing, because I was getting to know you that way."

"But it wasn't the worst sex of your life, right?" He'd made his expression so grave she had to laugh.

"I don't think I need to tell you that."

"Good. Because it was the best sex of mine. I mean, I know I don't really know you anymore. And I know I never *really* knew you that well when we were kids, despite us being in school together for twelve years."

"Plus kindergarten—thirteen years. Like cicadas," she whispered in a spooky voice, drumming her fingers along his forearm.

"I didn't let you know *me* well enough for that to happen. But if there's some version of love where you don't have to actually know the other person all that deeply…I feel that for you."

She blinked. "Wow."

"And it feels amazing."

She squeezed his hand. "So the next time you play Never Have I Ever and somebody says 'I've never had sex with someone I love'…?"

"Totally not drinking."

She smiled and stroked his knuckles, hummed a happy noise. "Daniel Barber…*making love*."

"Must be a Christmas miracle."

"Very Dickensian. I think that makes me the Ghost of Infatuation Past or something to your Ebenezer."

"We really ought to get some sleep," Daniel murmured, lips teasing her cheek. "Much as I never want this night to end."

"Yeah." She craned her neck, the clock on the nightstand telling her it was pushing four. "Oh, Jesus. We might want to rethink that six a.m. wake-up call."

"I'll get up when it's light out," he said through a yawn. "See what the road's looking like. We'll take it slow, and we'll probably make it home by dinnertime, if not in time for you to meet your brother at the station. Sorry."

"It's not your fault. And as bummed as that makes me, the stupid weather got us together. I can't be mad at that."

His laugh was a warm little hum. "No, me neither."

She turned over, spooning her back to his chest, smiling as his strong arm wrapped her up tight. "I'd say, 'See you in the morning,' but it's already morning."

"Say Merry Christmas instead."

"Indeed." She cleared her throat. "Thank you for my gift."

"Both of them."

She laughed, but he had that wrong. "Not the orgasms. Just you. Just us, getting to be this way. Thanks for being brave enough to come out and say what you did."

"Drunk enough, you mean."

"Semantics." Carrie yawned.

"Thank you," he whispered, sounding uncharacteristically earnest. "For…for all of this."

"My literal pleasure."

"Now I get to wake up next to you."

She smiled. "If we ever fall asleep."

"Night," he said, and kissed her hair.

"Morning," she returned, and settled her buzzing body against the calming heat of his strong one. "And Merry Christmas."

9

THEY GOT ON the road around eight in the morning, finding the asphalt blessedly—if inadequately—dusted with sand. It was still slick and the going slow. Daniel's knuckles were white, reflexes alert for the faintest tug of the wheel, the briefest slip of the tiny Fiat's tires. By the time they climbed back in after a quick lunch stop outside Eugene, he at least felt confident they'd survive to see their respective families.

The morning had been nice. He'd fought every self-defeating script programmed into his personality and forced himself not to shut down in the wake of all that soul bearing. It felt awkward and hurt a little in his chest, but he wouldn't trade it for the cold comfort of his usual armor.

He took a deep drink of the coffee they were sharing. Normally, he drank it black, but he had deferred to Carrie, and the creamy, sugary result was pretty disgusting. Yet he had to wonder if the memory of this trip just might change his preferences. There was something to be said for this sweetness.

"What do you think?" she asked. "Another five hours, with these roads?"

He set the cup back in the holder. "Maybe four if the ice eases up the farther north we get."

"Fingers crossed." After a pause, she amended that. "Not that this road trip isn't pretty nice in itself."

Nice? *Try the best gift I could have asked for.*

Though they made terrible time, the nearer they got to Grafton the better the roads became. The world seemed to thaw, just as Daniel had en route to finding himself so at home in easy small talk. He felt calm, for the first time in ages—and right at the moment he'd been anticipating dread and anxiety, as their hometown drew closer under a darkening sky.

AFTER A HALF hour of companionable silence, Carrie said, "You know, I bet we were supposed to be on the same flight to Portland. Leaving at seven-ten?"

Daniel nodded.

"Maybe we'd have wound up seated next to each other. Maybe fate had it in for us all along."

"How long are you in Grafton for?" he asked.

"I fly out the day after tomorrow. All the time I could get off, sadly. You?"

"Same." Three days had sounded like ages when he'd made the promise to his grandma, but seeing how he'd lost nearly an entire day, he was grateful for it now. "Early flight."

"Mine's not until dinnertime."

"You mind if I return the car at PDX?" Daniel asked. "It'll save me having to ask one of my parents for a lift. And spare me their company. And spare you the headache of telling the rental people we're returning it short a headlight and side-mirror and a load of paint."

"No problem. Shawn was planning on taking me."

"Cool."

"Actually, no doubt he'll want to go to the bar while we're both home. So tomorrow night I'll probably be playing des-ignated driver, in case you wanted to hang out at Paulie's, not drinking. Check out how old our fellow GHS alums have gotten."

"Maybe... Late, maybe. I, um, I'm going home mainly to spend time with my grandma. She doesn't think she's going to see another Christmas, so I may just hang out with her playing cards and watching movies."

"Oh, sure. Of course." As they passed by the big wooden sign, she read, "'Welcome to Grafton.'"

"But if my grandma goes to bed early, maybe I could swing by," Daniel added. Could be really weird, though, if Matt happened to be at the bar, or any of their old classmates, he thought as they drove past the high school. If people saw him and Carrie there together, the news would surely spread like a rash.

Whatever. It's time to start making some nice memories in this town for a change.

"We'll swap numbers," Carrie said. "I'll let you know what I end up doing."

"Sounds good."

She laughed softly. "And every thirteen years on Christmas, we'll return to the Evergreen Motor Inn, cicada-like, and resume this…whatever it is."

That got his pulse pounding, left his throat dry. He met her eyes for a moment, then looked back to the road, nervous.

"What?"

"We don't…I mean, we don't live *that* far apart, really, in the grand scheme of things. Maybe three hours' drive."

Carrie kept her voice light and level. "Hour and a half apiece if we met in the middle."

His chest filled. "Good old I-5. Maybe we could meet up in Modesto or wherever, sometime."

Did she have any clue how fast his heart was beating waiting those two seconds for her reply? It felt like a humming-bird between his ribs.

"What are you doing on New Year's Eve?" she asked.

And here he'd been hoping she'd want to see him in the next couple *months*. Next week? Shit, yes. "Nothing."

"I RSVP'd for a friend's party already. She has an amazing apartment with a view of the bay. Would you have any interest in coming up for that?"

He answered honestly. "You could invite me to come and pump your septic tank and I'd say yes."

She laughed, the best sound in the world. "I'll bear that in mind. And if parties aren't really your thing, I can just cancel. We could do whatever we wanted."

"No, I'd love to come."

He wanted to see where she lived and what her life was

like. He still wanted all the things he'd had when they'd both been living in this little town—a glimpse of her bedroom, a snoop through her bookshelves. He wanted to sit at her kitchen table or on her couch and drink coffee with her in the morning. Go out to eat with her. Shower with her. Run errands with her. Walk around her neighborhood or along the cold beach. Make a meal with her. Watch a movie. Take her to bed. Get taken there himself. He wanted to spend such a perfect January first with Carrie that the rest of the year could be complete misery and it wouldn't even matter.

"I ought to warn you," she said. "It's a one-bedroom."

He snorted. "Scandal. Also, this is all barring a fire, obviously."

"Sure."

"Though this time of year, luck's probably on my side."

"Let's hope California doesn't take a page out of western Oregon's book and order an ice storm."

"No kidding."

When he glanced her way, she was smiling, attention aimed forward as they drove through the town's center where the trees twinkled with white lights. He doubted he would've even noticed those lights without this woman beside him.

"You're still the prettiest girl I've ever seen," he told her, feeling naked in the nicest way.

She met his eyes with her dark ones and Daniel looked back to the road, feeling shy.

"Thanks."

He swallowed. "Sure."

"You probably need both hands on the wheel, huh?"

"Definitely."

She leaned over and rested her palm on his thigh. Daniel felt his neck and face flush with pleasure, and he hazarded a quick rub of her knuckles.

"Thanks for driving," Carrie said.

Daniel remembered the miles and miles of grit-messy

dangerous asphalt, the endless trees drooping and depressed under coats of ice. The speed limit-signs that had made a joke of their progress. The flat gray winter sky, now dark.

"Thanks for the best Christmas of my life," he replied. He punched the stereo button and filled their ridiculous little car with the bright chaos of pop music.

* * * * *

ALL NIGHT LONG

Debbi Rawlins

1

"HEY, WOULD YOU please keep it down?" Carly Wyatt glared at her coworker sitting across the gleaming mahogany conference table, but Mavis didn't even look up. She just kept humming "Silent Night" while she read the deposition in front of her.

Kevin, the newest paralegal to join the firm, was sitting next to Mavis. He tapped her shoulder and she yanked out an earbud. "The grouch wants you to hum to yourself."

Mavis automatically looked at Carly. Not Susan or Patti, neither of whom had been the embodiment of Christmas joy. Susan hadn't cracked a smile in a week. Not that Carly blamed her. The grueling fifteen-hour days searching for a tiny piece of evidence that could exonerate their client was getting to all of them. Maybe Carly most of all, but, dammit, she was supposed to be on vacation—her first in three years.

Working full-time as a paralegal while attending law school at night meant virtually no opportunities to go home. And now it seemed she'd be lucky to make it to Pittsburgh by New Year's Eve, much less Christmas.

"I said please," Carly muttered and dragged another file out of the rows of boxes stacked waist-deep along the glass wall, all courtesy of the Manhattan Assistant D.A.

The smug little jerk had bombarded them with paperwork at the last minute hoping they wouldn't find what they needed before returning to court the day after Christmas.

Sometimes she hated attorneys. Seriously. With all their courtroom theatrics and sneaky legal maneuverings. Sure, it was all for the good of the client. Yeah…yeah…she got that.

Or at least she'd better since she would be taking the bar in six months. Hopefully, she'd pass the exam the first go-round so she could be one of those despised lawyers and not the poor dope sitting here so bleary-eyed she could barely focus.

But then Susan was a first-year associate. That hadn't spared her from being thrown into the pit of overworked and underappreciated paralegals. Not unusual for first-years. They got dealt the grunt work. As for the paralegals, Carly was top dog. The senior partners, Mr. Abbott and Ms. Flynn, always demanded she work on their cases.

She doubted that would exempt her from paying her dues as a newbie attorney. If anything, she worried they'd still treat her like support staff and not consider her one of them. But Abbott and Flynn was an old, prominent Manhattan law firm so it was a risk she was willing to take. Assuming they didn't turn their noses up at her night-school law degree. At least she had Ryan Dunn in her corner. Last month he'd made equity partner and he'd sworn he would go to the mat for her when the time came.

"Am I the only one thinking about food?" Kevin asked, which had everyone glancing at the clock—7:30 p.m. It felt like midnight.

"We should order something." Mavis rose and stretched out her back. "I'm up for Thai or Chinese."

A pair of groans were cut off by the door opening.

Ryan stuck his head inside. "How's it coming?"

"Really?" Carly glared at him. "Either that was a brave or stupid question. I'm thinking the latter."

She heard some muffled chuckling but Ryan didn't seem amused. "I'd like a word with you," he said looking directly at her. "In private."

Sighing, Carly pushed to her feet, and tried not to think about how much her ass hurt from sitting so long. She supposed she shouldn't have said that in front of the others. Few people knew about her short fling with Ryan over a year ago. Or maybe she was kidding herself and everyone knew… Though he hadn't been her boss at the time, the mutual split wasn't particularly juicy gossip. They'd decided they were better off colleagues.

"Don't wait until I'm back to order dinner," she said, pausing to squeeze her tired feet into her heels. "Just get me something veg."

Kevin barked out a laugh. "What about the half-pound cheeseburger you wolfed down last night?"

"What about it?" she murmured, distracted by Ryan waiting for her in the hall.

Something was wrong.

She watched him through the glass, pacing and rubbing his left temple as if he'd forgotten they could all see him. Ryan prided himself on keeping cool under pressure.

"Hey," she said, closing the door behind her. "Your office?"

He stared past her into the conference room, where, she imagined, all eyes were on them. Without a word he turned and walked toward the elevators. The whole floor was quiet, the silence kind of eerie. Normally half the staff would still be working. But this close to Christmas a lot of employees had taken vacation. Like her. Except here she was, staring at the back of Ryan's head.

His office was on the next floor up, and the elevator door had barely closed when he turned to her with his charming Ivy League smile. "How would you like to get out of working on the Emerson case?"

Carly might've been amused if she wasn't so tired. "What's the catch?"

"No catch. I'm not letting you off scot-free. I have another task for you."

"Scot-free? I'm supposed to be on vacation." She realized the car hadn't moved and she jabbed at the button. *Scot-free.*

"I know. That's why I'm getting you out of that conference room and home for Christmas."

"You have my attention."

"Why the suspicious frown, Carly?" He nudged her chin

up, and she moved her head just enough to break contact. "Can't you believe I want to do something nice for you?"

"Frankly, no."

"That hurts."

"You'll get over it. What do you want, Ryan?"

"I need you to fly to Chicago."

"Chicago? Are you kidding?"

The elevator door slid open. Olivia was still at the reception desk. Carly managed a smile as she walked briskly past the older woman. He was crazy if he thought she was flying all the way to Chicago four days before Christmas.

"Do me a favor, Carly, don't talk," he said once they were in his office and he closed the door. "Hear me out before you say anything."

"Don't talk? Really?" She folded her arms across her chest. "You thought that would soften me up?"

He sighed. "Look, this is a quick, no-brainer assignment. I need you to get a couple signatures. You fly in, fly out. Go straight to Pittsburgh on the firm's dime."

She'd been dreading the seven-hour trip, but a bus ticket was all she could afford. "Why not use a courier?"

"I'm trying to give you a way out."

Carly relaxed her arms. She wanted to believe him, but Ryan wasn't known for his charity. And he knew better than to give her special treatment. "It's not fair to everyone else."

Shrugging, he went to his glass-and-chrome desk. Files and briefs covered the surface. Quite a mess considering he was a neat freak. "They aren't supposed to be on vacation."

True, which made it easy to rationalize accepting the offer. Though she wasn't convinced being nice was Ryan's only motive. She liked him as a friend, and so far he'd been a decent boss, but he was also ambitious and tended to look out for number one.

"First class," Carly said. "Make it a first-class ticket and you have a deal."

He looked up with amusement. "I can't approve that."

"Sure you can."

The charming smile was gone. "All right. But you have to leave first thing in the morning."

"I can make it by noon."

"Jesus, Carly, I'm giving you a gift here." He stabbed a finger in the air, vaguely pointing in the direction of the elevator. "You want to spend Christmas Eve in that conference room?"

"We could find what we need in the next five minutes."

"Maybe," he said in a cocky tone.

They both knew the odds of that happening were slim to none, but she waited him out. He'd given in too easily on the first-class ticket. Whatever this errand, it was too important to haggle over.

"One at the latest," he ground out while tugging his tie loose. "Check flights and get back to me. Now."

She'd never seen him so disheveled, so worried. "Whose signatures am I getting?"

"Jackson Carrington. Both senior and junior," he said, averting his eyes. "You understand why I want to keep this quiet."

A sick feeling came over her. The sale would be final and the switch-over scheduled to happen at the end of the year. All documents should've been signed and filed by now. "What else should I know?"

"No one's returning my calls. Carrington senior has been anxious to sell from the beginning. I assumed the son was on board. He's the company's only counsel so he's handling things on their end. He should've sent everything back by now." Ryan sighed. "I don't know what to think."

This wasn't good. Abbott and Flynn represented the buyer, Luxury Lighting, also the firm's third largest client. Ryan would be crucified if he messed up this sale. She checked the time. "Look, I'll take the first flight out I can get tomorrow," she said. "But why aren't you going yourself?"

"I considered it. Frankly, you're the better bet." He paused. "Now, don't get in my face for this, but I noticed the way Carrington eyed you last time they were here."

"The old man?"

"The son."

Her heart thumped. Jackson Carrington was hot. And rich. Half the office had come to a standstill when he'd shown up in Reception. She'd exchanged a few words with him. Strictly work-related. But other than that, he hadn't paid any attention to her. "Are you crazy? He barely knows I exist."

Ryan laughed. "Ah, Carly, that's one of the things I like about you…. Yeah, Carrington did more than notice. Trust me."

2

By 6:00 P.M., the Carrington Lamps's employee Christmas party was in full swing. No one seemed to mind that they were still at the plant. Over a hundred people were in attendance, some of them spouses, most of them decked out in their holiday finest. So many sequins, so much velvet…

So much perfume…

A cloying whiff of jasmine wafted up to where Jack Carrington stood on the twelfth-floor balcony of the executive offices and he reared back. He had to admit, whoever had decorated had done quite a job of transforming the eleventh floor.

It wasn't used for much—the supervisors' cubicles and displaying the original equipment his great-grandfather had used back in the early '30s. Mostly, though, the floor served as a buffer between the factory noise from the lower stories and the executive offices.

White lights and blue-and-gold ornaments glittered from three giant Christmas trees blocking off the cubicles. Fresh garland and large foil-wrapped poinsettias had been strategically placed to hide cords and areas of neglect. In the corner a DJ played a mix of oldies and Christmas carols. Two portable bars had been stocked with premium liquor. The champagne flowed freely, not the cheap stuff either…Jack had seen to that.

His father had been outraged over the top-grade prime rib and seafood Jack had approved for the party. He smiled. Remembering those little things would help him get through the evening.

That, and getting smashed.

He held up his glass. Not much left of his second scotch. He drained the last of it when he saw Eli climbing the stairs with a refill sitting on his tray. The waiter was no dummy. He'd been quick to figure out Jack would be the person passing out tips at the end of the evening, and the man had been shrewdly attentive.

"Thank you, Eli," Jack said, exchanging his empty for the fresh drink.

"My pleasure, sir. May I bring you some hors d'oeuvres?"

"No, thanks." He needed to start mingling. Someone from the family should be out there pretending everything was fine.

The thought brought an acute tightness to his chest. It wasn't that he didn't like interacting with the employees. Quite the opposite. He'd known most of these people since he was old enough to talk. Some of his best childhood memories were from summers he'd spent hanging around the plant, asking a million questions and learning how to run the machinery. How could he laugh and joke and pretend these loyal Carrington employees of twenty, thirty years weren't about to lose their jobs?

Picturing the stack of pink slips sitting in his desk drawer made him feel sick. Tonight they were partying. The day after Christmas, their lives would change forever.

All because Carrington Lamps's biggest competitor had made an obscenely lucrative offer that his father had been unable to refuse. As if he wasn't already filthy rich. But then Jack was doing all right himself. His share from the sale meant the rest of his life could be one big party. That was partly why he hadn't objected when negotiations began five months ago. No room for him to be pious now.

"Sir?"

Jack looked at Eli, who'd apparently asked him something. What, he had no idea. Jack glanced at the full glass in his hand. After this he had to take it easy, or go from slightly buzzed to drunk. Which might end up being the goal. Just not this early. "Don't bring me any more scotch."

"Champagne, perhaps?"

"Nothing for now."

Eli nodded and turned for the stairs.

Jack was about to follow him when he saw a tall shapely brunette step out of the elevator.

Carly Wyatt?

Here in Chicago?

He blinked, in case the alcohol was playing tricks on him.

Definitely Carly. He wasn't sure about the last name, but he had no doubt she was the smokin' hot paralegal who worked for Abbott and Flynn in Manhattan.

Huh. So they'd sent her...

Interesting.

The carol ended, another one started and Jack smiled. Yes, it was indeed starting to feel a lot like Christmas.

He watched her survey the room, her shiny hair brushing her shoulders with each turn of her head. Her conservative navy blue suit had to be Abbott and Flynn standard issue. Visiting their offices was like attending an undertakers' convention. Everyone wore traditional dark suits, their power ties the only thing distinguishing them in a sea of blue and gray.

Not Carly, though, she'd skipped the tie and the two top buttons of her blouse, and was making her mark with a pair of red high heels. God bless her. Man, she had great legs.

Ted from Purchasing approached her. It figured he'd be the first guy in line. Jack had to give him credit...Ted never let little things, like being outclassed, or mustard on his white shirt, stop him from going for the gold.

Reggie and Leo, two stocky machinists, stepped up right beside Ted, who, with a long face, turned and pointed at Jack.

Carly lifted her gaze to him.

And Jack lifted his glass to her...before tossing the scotch back with a single gulp.

Dumbass move.

Though he imagined he'd looked pretty cool. Very Bond-like, minus the tux.

The asinine thought was reason enough for him to stay off the booze.

Without hesitation she weaved her way through a group from Accounting and made it to the stairs. He'd only seen her twice before and both times her hair had been neatly pinned up in a twist. He liked it down much better, all bouncy and shiny as she hurried up the stairs, swiping back her long bangs.

"Mr. Carrington?" Leaving the last step she put out her hand. "Carly Wyatt from Abbott and Flynn."

"From where?"

She gave him a small tolerant smile. "I promise not to keep you from your party. I only need—"

He caught her hand and drew her close. She let out a startled gasp, her caramel-colored eyes widening. "The employees don't know yet," he said in a hushed voice, the music and rowdy laughter nearly drowning him out and making a mockery of his warning.

She swept a gaze over the festive crowd below. "Clearly," she said, then reared back with a look of horror. "I wasn't judging."

He glanced longingly into his empty glass. With his luck, he wouldn't get drunk even if he tried. "How about a drink? We have some very good champagne."

"How about we stick to business?" Carly took another step back. "All I want is the signed contract and you'll be rid of me."

"I doubt that."

"Believe me, I have no desire to hang around. In fact, I have a cab waiting."

"Ah." Most of her lip gloss was gone. He studied her mouth, trying to decide if those lush lips were her best feature. Not an easy decision. Not with those arresting almond-shaped eyes. "You should let the cab go."

With an impatient glance at her watch, she sighed. "You've

had the contract for over a week and, since we haven't heard otherwise, I assume everything is in order." She paused, her eyes narrowing. "If there is a problem you should've notified Mr. Dunn before now."

Ryan Dunn. He was a smart, competent attorney, but Jack didn't like the guy. Too smooth. Too smug. Jack knew the type. Hell, he'd gone to Yale Law School a year behind Dunn. Obviously he hadn't remembered Jack, which was no surprise. Dunn had always been self-absorbed. "Was it his idea to send you?"

"Mr. Dunn?" Carly blinked, then glanced away. "Luxury Lighting is his client."

"No need to be defensive. I was just curious."

"So…do you have the contract?"

"Locked in my desk." He spotted Eli helping a waitress set up the buffet. Jack got his attention and motioned him upstairs.

"Do you like Seruga caviar?"

"Never had it." She shifted her briefcase from her right hand to her left.

"Here. Let me take that for you…"

"No. Thank you." Carly moved out of reach. "The contract, Mr. Carrington?"

Eli showed up with two flutes of champagne on his tray. "What can I do for you, sir?"

Jack reached in his pocket for some cash, and peeled off a hundred-dollar bill. "There's a taxi waiting outside. You mind paying the driver off for me?"

"My pleasure."

"Wait." Carly sputtered. "You can't. That's my cab."

Jack thought a moment. She'd probably come straight from the airport. He pulled off another hundred and passed both bills to Eli. "Give the driver a nice tip," Jack said, ignoring her and lifting the flutes off the tray. "And keep the rest for yourself."

Eli grinned. "Consider it done."

"Stop." She waited until she had Eli's full attention before she turned to Jack. "You can't just— No. The taxi stays."

"Relax, Carly. We have plenty of cabs in Chicago."

"I have a plane to catch."

"You'd leave without the contract?"

Temper flashed in her eyes. Lowering her lashes, she took a moment to compose herself. "Please tell me this is a bad dream," she said, sighing.

Jack wasn't going to lie. He offered her champagne instead, but she shook her head.

"I have a bag," she muttered, sounding cross and defeated. "In the trunk."

Luggage, huh? So she wasn't returning to New York. Probably on her way to spend Christmas somewhere else. Jack didn't want to ruin her holiday, but he wasn't about to let emotion dictate his decision. Except that's exactly what he was doing. Allowing guilt and sentiment to interfere with a deal he'd fully endorsed.

Meeting over fancy dinners and negotiating behind closed doors, the terms of sale had seemed perfectly fine. Or at least they hadn't motivated him to object too loudly. The name, the equipment, the building would all go to Luxury Lighting. Two managers and four salespeople would be guaranteed positions. But only if they were willing to relocate to New Jersey. The Chicago plant would be closed and the remainder of the employees would get nothing but a month's severance pay and the Carrington family's heartfelt thanks.

What bullshit.

And yet, between bad jokes and sips of well-aged Remy Martin, he'd agreed to everything.

"Mr. Carrington?" Carly was studying him with a look of concern.

She really did have extraordinary eyes. A light brown

warmed by flecks of gold. And her skin was as smooth as silk. Even standing this close to her he couldn't see a single flaw.

He noticed that Eli was still awaiting instructions. "When's your flight?" Jack asked her.

A hopeful expression brightened her face. "In two and a half hours."

Ah, hell…why had he bothered asking? He wasn't ready to put pen to paper, and he doubted she'd leave without getting the contract signed. Either way he was going to disappoint her. And piss off everyone involved.

Except Eli, of course. The guy was going to make out like a bandit.

Sighing, Jack returned a flute to the tray and reached into his pocket for a twenty. "Grab her bag, too, would you?"

3

CARLY GLARED AT Jack Carrington. She didn't care that he had sexy blue-green eyes or that he was tall enough that at 5'11" in heels she didn't feel like a giant. Or that he had broad shoulders, a cute dimple and a ridiculously attractive smile.

Yes, so what? He was hot…crazy hot. That wasn't news.

And that stupid notion Ryan had about Jack being attracted to her? She didn't buy it. It was just Ryan's desperate attempt to manipulate her. Hoping she'd leap at the chance to go cozy up to Jack. Ryan should know her better than that. Sure she might like to look, but she wasn't about to get stupid over a man. Carly had already made the mistake of thinking a woman's looks and social status didn't matter. Different guy, different time, but the lesson had sliced deep enough to last a lifetime.

So, hot as Jack was, right now she wanted to strangle him.

She took a deep breath as she tried to formulate her next move. That he was being a stubborn ass helped calm her down. She'd spent half the plane ride worried she'd make a fumbling fool of herself once they were face-to-face.

The last time she'd seen him, Jack had merely smiled at her and she'd spilled part of her latte. He probably hadn't noticed, but dammit, she'd had to walk around with a brown blotch on her blouse for the rest of the day.

"I see you're upset and I'm sorry you were put out," Jack said, giving her that winning smile. "I had no way of knowing you would show up here."

"You didn't return the contract. Or Ryan's calls. What did you think would happen?"

He studied her for a moment. "You're right. That was very

unprofessional of me. But I did leave him a message an hour ago. Does that earn me a little forgiveness?"

Mesmerized by his eyes, Carly stared a moment too long. His words finally sank in and she dug her cell out of her pocket. No message from Ryan. "Did Mr. Dunn get back to you?"

"Not yet."

Now that she thought about it, odd that she hadn't heard from him since she'd left New York. Nervous as he'd been about meeting the deadline, it was a miracle he wasn't bombarding her with annoying texts or calls. "What was the message?"

"I told him there was a holdup, and I'd get back to him."

"That's it? No explanation?"

Jack shrugged and took an unhurried sip of champagne.

She drew in a deep breath. She hated dealing with self-centered men used to getting their own way. "You can't up the asking price at this stage. I'm sure you know that," she said, netting herself a wince of disgust.

"Not everything is about money, Ms. Wyatt."

"Sure, I guess," she said, shrugging. "Easy to be cavalier if you already have it."

He lifted a brow at her, his expression pure amusement.

"I'm sorry," she mumbled, feeling heat surge up her neck. "That was inappropriate."

"No problem." His gaze lingered on her mouth, until he got distracted by the excited whoops coming from the party below.

Waiters and waitresses were setting large platters of crab, jumbo shrimp and lobster on the buffet table. Another man wearing a white coat and chef hat was carving slabs of prime rib while people started grabbing plates and forming a line.

"Hey, Jack." A big barrel-chested man wearing a red bow tie and matching suspenders gave him a thumbs-up. "You went all out, buddy. Like I've always said, you're the best."

Jack lifted his glass and gave the man a strained smile.

Others called up to him, offering thanks or requesting that he join the party. They all referred to him as Jack…as if he was one of them. Except he wasn't looking so jolly.

In fact, he looked…what…sad?

Huh. What was up with that?

She regarded him for a moment, as he stood watching everyone with a peculiar fondness, much like a teacher presiding over his favorite class for the last time.

Well, damn. This, she hadn't expected. Had he changed his mind? Did Jack Carrington not want to sell the company? Of course they couldn't back out now.

"Mr. Carrington?"

"It's Jack," he said. "Call me Jack. Everyone does."

"And your father?"

"Oh, he's definitely Mr. Carrington."

They had a moment…briefly exchanging smiles, their eyes meeting.

How easy it would be to lose herself in those blue-green depths. The flutter in her tummy settled into an ache. She had to stay focused. "Where is your father? I'd like to speak with him."

"Good luck with that. I have no idea where he is." Jack continued to watch people pile food on their plates. "He should be out there shaking hands."

"Has he signed the contract?"

"No."

She hadn't expected that response at all. "You're both holdouts?"

"Who said anything about holding out?" he asked, a glimmer of challenge in his eyes.

"You're right. You said there was a holdup." She paused. "You really don't know where he is?"

"I haven't seen the new receptionist," he said, surveying the crowd. "My guess is they're making merry in an empty office." His mouth curved into a wicked smile. "She's half his age and not screwing him for his looks. Can you imagine her face when she finds out about the sale?"

Carly refused to react. Why give him the satisfaction? His words slowly registered. It sounded as if he expected the sale to proceed. So maybe she'd misjudged the situation.

"Ah, here comes Eli with your bag. We'll put it in my office."

She glanced at the waiter making his way to the stairs, the old battered canvas bag in tow. Most of the employees were too interested in the buffet to notice him. The few who did, and of course they were guys, eyed the overnight bag and had no trouble jumping to the wrong conclusion. She ignored the big goofy grins aimed at her and Jack. "Look, I need to know. Is there any chance I'll be catching a plane tonight?"

He didn't even try to look apologetic. "You really should try the champagne."

God, she wanted to scream. She'd promised herself she'd stay professional even if it killed her. Death was looking more imminent. "Let's cut the crap, okay? Tell me what it would take for me to get out of here with a signed contract."

His single lifted brow did interesting things to her fluttering heart. Which pissed her off. She knew it was purely a physical response, but she wished her body would knock it off.

He ran his gaze down the front of her blazer to her knee-length skirt, then to her legs. She folded her arms across her chest, waited until he returned to her face, and with a pointed glare dared him to say something suggestive.

"I was just admiring your...suit." He smiled, reminding her of a precocious child testing his parents' limits. "It's very Abbott and Flynn."

"I'll take that as a compliment."

"You should," he said with a straight face. "Absolutely."

Against her will, she felt her lips lifting at the corners, and wondered if the man ever failed to get his way. Charm, good looks, smarts and money...sometimes life just wasn't fair.

"Where would you like me to put this, sir?"

She turned to Eli and reached for her bag at the same time Jack did. No contest. Eli gave it up to the man who'd been tipping him as if cash grew in his pocket.

"Is this all you have?" Jack hefted the bag after Eli left to get more champagne. "It's not very heavy."

She glanced at the old blue bag that she'd had since college. It had never looked shabbier than it did right now. No matter, she couldn't afford a new one. Any extra money she could scrape together would go toward another boring "Abbott and Flynn" suit. She might not be an attorney yet, but to get ahead she believed it helped to look the part.

"Where are you going after this?" he asked and gestured toward double glass doors. "Skiing?"

"Oh, sure." She gave him a dry look. "Aspen awaits."

"Sarcasm? That was a perfectly legitimate question."

"In your circles maybe." It was freezing outside. Snow was on the ground, yet Jack's face and forearms exposed by his rolled-back sleeves were tan. Obviously he'd recently visited someplace warm and sunny. How nice for him. "Some of us actually work for a living."

"Ah, but you're not judging."

She mentally winced. "Pittsburgh," she said, refusing to look at him. "I'm on my way to Pittsburgh."

He reached around and opened the door before she could. "To spend Christmas with your boyfriend? Your family?"

"Actually, it looks like I might be spending it with you."

Jack laughed. "I can live with that."

Squeezing past him, she got an intoxicating whiff of his musky scent. It wasn't cologne. "My family's in Pittsburgh," she said. "And so is Brent, my boyfriend." She threw in the lie for good measure. "I haven't made it home for Christmas in three years. And now Brent's being deployed to Afghanistan. Oh, but please, don't feel guilty."

He searched her face, his eyes narrowing slightly. "Why should I? I didn't ask you to come."

God, he was really something. He didn't know she'd slipped in the lie, though Brent had been her boyfriend once and he was being deployed, so really, she wasn't being completely dishonest. The point was, the story should've had Jack feeling some remorse. All she got from him was a blank expression as he indicated she should go right.

Voices came from the opposite hall. Carly hesitated, wondering if he was steering her away from his father. She felt pressure at the small of her back. It was Jack's hand. He moved it lower, just a tiny bit, but enough to make her hold her breath. The bastard was trying to distract her. It had almost worked. Moving out of reach, she turned toward the voices. "I hear your father."

"No, you don't. That's my uncle, who's also the controller. But he can't help you. Harvey's my mom's brother." Jack smiled. "Wrong side of the family. Though I'd be happy to introduce you to him if you like."

She was beginning to regret passing up the champagne. Although bubbly tended to give her headaches. Maybe because she'd only had the cheap stuff. Her phone signaled she had a text and before she looked to see who it was, she sent up a heartfelt prayer to let it be Ryan telling her to forget the whole thing and head to Pittsburgh.

It was Mavis. They'd found the elusive memo so the team had celebrated with a round of tequila shots, then left for the holidays. Oh, and everyone wished Carly a Merry Christmas.

She bit off a curse, and texted Mavis to ask if she'd seen Ryan.

Yep, this week would surely top her best-vacation-ever list. Though she had every intention of getting the days back and tacked on to next year. Assuming she still had a job.

"Bad news?"

She looked up into Jack's amused face. This was all a game to him. "May I speak freely—off the record, so to speak?"

"By all means."

"You're an ass."

He didn't seem the least bit put off, even though she already regretted the rash words. After a quick glance toward the voices, he urged her to his office at the end of the hall. Once he'd closed the door, he asked, "Was that Ryan?"

"No." While his office was smaller and less showy than she'd expected, the breathtaking view of the Chicago skyline was a total surprise.

"Whatever happens, I won't let him use you as a scapegoat. I can promise you that much."

She turned away from the window. "What are you talking about? Ryan wouldn't do that."

Jack briefly met her eyes before looking away. Taking his time, he set her bag at the end of a burgundy leather couch, then glanced at a message slip sitting on his desk.

A knot began to form in her stomach. He knew something, she suddenly realized, something important that she didn't know but probably should. While Jack was distracted, or pretending to be, she texted Ryan.

She kept it short. **CALL ME!**

Carly never used all caps and Ryan knew that. If he ignored her, then she'd start worrying in earnest.

After slipping her phone into her pocket, she checked out Jack's office. The furnishings were tasteful yet simple—an end table with a signature Carrington lamp, a rich dark cherry desk and credenza, a matching bookcase filled with law books. On the wall behind his desk hung a silver-framed picture of the original factory that must've been taken in the '30s.

"That's my great-grandfather on the right," he said. "The other man is his brother. Jasper helped start the business but he died young, in his late twenties. So mainly it was Granddad who made Carrington Lamps a success. No man worked harder than him. He was really something, still coming to the office into his late eighties. Not only did he know the name of every employee, he remembered their birthdays."

"Did you get to know him?"

"I was ten when he passed away. He'd give me odd jobs and pay me with a silver dollar for each one I completed. I still have them in a piggy bank."

Carly laughed. "Seriously?"

"What?" He sounded offended. "He taught me a good work ethic. It's too easy to hand kids money."

"I agree. I was just trying to imagine you with a piggy bank. What color was it?"

He came close enough that his shoulder brushed hers and whispered, "Pink. I still have it. Tell anyone and there'll be consequences."

His warm breath glided down the side of her neck, making her pulse jump. He kept moving, walking past her. She had no idea what he was...

Apparently she hadn't heard the knock. He opened the door to Eli standing in the hall holding a champagne bottle and two glasses.

"Thank you," Jack said, taking the bubbly from him. "And if anyone asks for me?"

Eli grinned. "I haven't seen you."

4

"WHAT ARE YOU DOING?" Carly's hands went to her hips as she watched him set down the glasses, then open the bottle.

Her blouse wasn't tight but with her elbows out the silk strained across her breasts and he almost lost the cork. "Take off your jacket," he said casually. "Kick off your shoes. Relax."

"I'm not sitting here, drinking champagne with you."

"Fine. Stand if you like."

"Oh, was that supposed to be funny? Was I supposed to laugh? Sorry." She let out a fake snort. "You know, I'm sure many women find you adorable. Just not all of us."

Jack's mood slipped. He got that she was irritated, flying out here for nothing, but he sure hadn't asked for that remark. He filled both flutes anyway. "Then what are you going to do? Find a hotel?"

Her mouth tightening, she briefly glanced at her phone. "I'm going to ask around for your father."

"I wish you wouldn't do that."

"Why?"

Jack sighed at the smug lift of her brows. "Normally he says a few words and does some handshaking. I would rather not point out his absence."

She narrowed her eyes, her suspicion slipping the longer she studied him. "Have there been rumors about the sale?"

"None. The poor saps won't know what hit them." He downed a good part of his drink before he remembered it was champagne and not scotch. Hell, he wouldn't be doing that again. "For what it's worth, I've left him three messages." He carried the glass to the window and stared out at the lights. Only half the skyline was visible but it was better than looking at another old building. "I love the view at night. The daytime, not so much. I'm sure you noticed this isn't the best neighborhood."

Carly came to stand beside him. Seeing her reflection in the glass and watching her nibble at her lip reminded him of the first time he'd seen her at Abbott and Flynn's. With her confidence and no-nonsense attitude, he'd assumed she was an associate, just one of many attorneys in their sizeable stable. She'd been wearing a dreary brown suit and low-heeled shoes that she'd kicked under her desk. The horrified expression on her face when she'd realized she was walking around in stocking feet had been priceless.

The moment in itself hadn't been enough for him to have thought about her so many times since. Or have an X-rated dream that had kept him hard through an early quality-control meeting. For the life of him he couldn't pin down what it was about her that got to him. She was attractive but not a classic beauty. Although a woman's looks weren't all he cared about.

At least not since his horny teens. A woman had to have confidence, intelligence, a sense of humor and be independent to hold his attention.

Or a killer body and any two of the above.

"It is a great view," she said quietly. "You're lucky no one put up a skyscraper across the street."

"Luck had nothing to do with it." Even on the outskirts of the city every building around them was newer and taller. "I own that piece of land right there."

She looked at him, then at the vacant lot that took up half a block. "Is it part of the sale?"

"No. It belongs to me, personally."

"What do you plan to do with it?"

He shrugged. "Originally, nothing. The whole point of buying it was to preserve the view. If the sale goes through, I won't give a crap about the lot then."

"Technically, the sale has gone through," she reminded him.

He ignored her softly spoken words and continued to stare at his piece of the skyline. "I bought it six years ago when the developer defaulted. Someday I'll make a nice profit." He drained his glass. "I guess I should go mingle. Come with me if you want. Who knows? Maybe the old man will show up."

"Jack?" She touched his hand just as he turned away. "Were you always against selling?"

"No." He could see she was hoping for more, but he left it at that and grabbed the champagne.

"If you know right now you aren't going to sign, will you at least be honest and tell me?"

He paused, holding the bottle aloft. "I don't know. That's the truth. Either way, it would be irresponsible for me to sign anything while I'm inebriated. So no, you won't be leaving with a signed contract tonight."

"Are you really drunk?"

After thinking for a moment he said, "I prefer the term *inebriated*."

She watched him position the bottle, and gasped when he started to pour. "Well, don't—"

Aware she was hoping he wouldn't drink any more, he refilled his glass anyway. "Like I said, tonight's already a lost cause." He held up the second flute he'd poured earlier for her but she shook her head.

No use letting it go to waste...

"Wait." She caught his arm just as the rim touched his lip. "I changed my mind," she said, taking the glass from him.

His laughter was met with a glare. He really wasn't drunk. As he'd suspected, it was going to be one of those nights that a mildly pleasant buzz would be it for him.

But watching her try to circumvent his drinking all evening? That could be entertaining.

Damn, but he wanted to kiss her. She had a wide mouth and her lips were naturally pink. He liked that she wore minimal makeup. He returned his gaze to her lips. Okay, maybe he was a little drunk because he was seriously starting to fixate on her mouth.

"Whatever you're thinking…I don't like it," she said, inching back and staring at him as if she expected him to pounce.

"Are you sure?"

"No." She sighed. "I mean, yes," she amended and took a big, and probably unintentional, sip. And then blinked at the glass. "Wow."

"Good stuff, right?"

She gave him a grudging nod. "I could get used to it."

"Now, a smart woman like yourself has to be wondering what else you could be missing out on."

Carly let out a loud bark of laughter. "In your dreams."

"Yes, sadly that, too." Jack smiled. "But we won't go there." He presented his arm, which, predictably, she ignored. "Shall we go downstairs?"

She glanced around. "I'll leave my briefcase and coat here with my bag."

"Your jacket, too," he said, nodding at her navy blazer. "It's a party, not a funeral. And while you're at it, unfasten another button on that blouse."

"Right. Sure thing. Remember what I said about you being an ass?"

"If you want to be my date, sweetheart, you'll have to be a little nicer."

"Your—" Her eyes widened. "Oh, my God, you are drunk."

"Everyone will be curious. Can't tell them why you're really here, now can we?" He slipped his arm around her shoulders.

She stiffened but didn't pull away. Or slap him. So he took a chance…

And went in for the kiss.

CARLY'S BREATH CAUGHT. Jack Carrington was about to lay one on her. It was nuts and unprofessional, and yet she didn't know how she felt about it, though she supposed she should object. Or duck.

But those damn sexy eyes of his were full of heat and promise and she could feel the tension coursing through his body. Could feel her heartbeat quicken in response.

"If you're going to run, better do it now," he whispered, his warm lips brushing the corner of her mouth.

She didn't move. Didn't even breathe. He slid a hand behind her neck and her lids started to drift closed.

With sudden clarity his words sank in. He was playing her and she'd almost fallen for it.

Carly forced herself to look directly into his eyes. "Stop," she said before she humiliated herself further. "Right now."

Abruptly, he drew back, looking somewhat stunned. "I apologize. Clearly I misread the signals."

"You're not going to get rid of me. So get over it."

His gaze narrowed. "Not my objective," he said, the amusement slowly returning to his face. "Not even close."

He seemed earnest enough but it was the trace of relief in his voice that had her reassessing the situation. He was a little drunk. Maybe all he'd wanted was to kiss her. Or any other woman within arm's reach.

She glanced down at the front of his gray slacks. Or maybe he was just horny and hoping for more than a kiss. He sure wasn't faking that bulge.

Her hand automatically went to her throat. As if that would help with her difficulty swallowing. Whatever tiny bit of sense she had left was slipping away. She focused on his shoes, then a piece of carpet lint. But she could feel him watching her.

A blush flamed in her chest and surged toward her cheeks. Luckily she didn't have the type of skin that turned red even though she felt as if she'd stepped into a sauna.

Much as she hated giving him the satisfaction, she had to lose the jacket or broil. Turning her back to him, she set down her glass, then started shrugging out of the blazer. His hands were suddenly on her shoulders, and he helped her out of the stifling wool.

While he draped her blazer over the couch, she fastened the second button of her blouse. She left the top one alone. As soon as he turned to her she saw that he'd noticed her petty act of rebellion. But she ignored his faint smile.

He picked up the champagne. "No sense wasting this. Let's top off before we join the party."

"I'm good. Thanks."

Shrugging, he filled his flute almost to the brim.

Oh, great. He'd never sober up. "I changed my mind. Save me some."

She found her glass, and polished off the last sip before letting him refill it. Half the bottle was already gone. How had that happened?

He took in her cream-colored blouse, his gaze lingering briefly on her breasts. "Not that I don't appreciate the view," he said, and gave a nod, "but you should probably keep that one buttoned."

She looked down. The large gap left no doubt her bra was pale pink, lacy and a demi cup. And the button wasn't unfastened. It was missing. She fisted the front of the blouse together and squinted at the plush beige carpet.

"What's wrong?"

"The button...I lost it."

"Here? You sure?"

"Um, if I'd lost it earlier, I think you might have noticed."

Jack grinned. "Good point."

"What are you staring at? *Missing* means you won't find it *there*." She tightened her fist and hoped she wasn't totally ruining the silk.

"I was checking the other buttons so I know what color to look for."

Made sense, but she wasn't feeling particularly reasonable at the moment. This was one of her favorite blouses. And the most expensive. She'd wanted to impress Jack. God, she was such a dope.

"This is your fault," she said, kicking off her heels and dropping to the floor.

"How?"

"If you'd had the contract ready I wouldn't still be here."

"Oh, so if you'd lost the button at the airport that would've been better?" Jack lowered himself to a crouch beside her. "You don't see the flaw in your logic?"

Carly's arm bumped his thigh. "Why are you here?"

"Because it's my office?"

"I meant—" She flapped a hand toward the bookcase and stole a peek at the fabric molding his muscled thigh. The man clearly wasn't afraid to work up a sweat. Sports? Or gym? "Go check over there. I've got this area covered."

"Don't you have another blouse in your bag?"

"Nothing appropriate." She crawled the few feet to his desk and looked underneath. The thick carpeting cushioned her knees, though she was more concerned with not trashing her hose. No luck. The extra small button with a creamy pearl finish was going to be a bitch to spot against the beige carpet.

It occurred to her that Jack was awfully quiet. She glanced at the bookcase, then behind her. He hadn't moved.

He was exactly where she'd left him. Crouched down and staring at her rear end.

5

"WHERE THE HELL have you been, Jacko?" Norm set his drink down on the table next to a plate overflowing with shrimp.

"No. Don't get up." Sighing, Jack watched the veteran shop steward jump to his feet. For a big guy he was quick.

He threw his burly arms around Jack and lifted him off the ground in a bone-crushing hug. "Where you been hiding? Have you seen the spread? I can't believe the old man sprang for all this stuff." He set Jack and his bruised ego back down. "Fifty bucks says he doesn't know. You did this, didn't you, Jacko?"

His fault, Jack thought, refusing to look at Carly as he tucked his shirt back in and pushed a hand through his disheveled hair. He knew better than to approach Norm after he'd had a few.

"So I take it you haven't seen him recently," Jack said, then glanced at Carly, who Norm was staring at as if he'd never seen a woman before. But then, so were the other six employees sitting at the table.

Norm's bushy eyebrows lowered. "You with Jack?"

"I am." She offered her hand. "Carly Wyatt."

She gave a small start when Norm's grip swallowed everything up to her wrist, but she held on to a smile.

He let her go and turned to his table companions. "What did I tell you guys? After that magazine came out I knew our boy would finally find himself a girlfriend."

"Ah, Jesus. That's enough." Jack had expressly forbidden the employees to bring up the subject. Ever. Why had he expected them to actually listen to their boss? He tugged at Carly's arm but of course she refused to give up her front-row seat.

"For heaven's sake, Norm," Evelyn from Payroll said with a dismissive sniff. "You've got rocks for brains if you think Jack ever needed help finding a girlfriend."

"Oh, yeah. Rocks, huh?" Norm rubbed his hands together with glee. "George, you owe me twenty. Same goes for you, Juan," he said to the two young machinists who were already digging into their pockets.

"What magazine?"

Everyone turned to Carly. She looked curious and far too mischievous. Living in Manhattan, she wouldn't have seen the article.

"She's kidding." Jack slid an arm around her waist and pulled her against his side. "Come on, sweetheart."

He'd caught her off guard. She leaned into him and her blouse puckered where a safety pin served as the lost button. He doubted anyone but him heard the soft gasp that parted her lips. Or saw the tip of her tongue slip out to moisten them a second before she met his eyes.

She gave him a sexy smile that dialed up his hopes for the night. Then she turned back to the table. "Someone tell me about the magazine. I'm dying of curiosity."

Norm slapped him on the back so hard he let go of Carly. "Jacko here was voted Chicago's sexiest man alive."

"You always get it wrong." Evelyn shook her head with disgust. "He's Chicago's second most eligible bachelor."

Jack sighed. "Thank you, everyone, for respecting my wishes that you never bring up the subject ever again." He dreaded looking at Carly but that was inevitable. He doubted she'd skip the opportunity to give him grief.

She looked stunned. And maybe even a little disappointed, which he didn't get.

"Didn't you know about it?" Evelyn asked, frowning at Carly. "The magazine came out two months ago. The local news did a feature on him."

"Well, that was about the time we met, right?" Carly

smiled at him and then at the group. "And unfortunately for us, I live in Manhattan."

"Oh, that's terrible." Evelyn clucked her tongue, while the rest of the gang shook their heads and made sympathetic noises.

"Any chance that could change?" Norm asked. "You can't be seeing much of each other with all the hours Jack works."

Carly jerked a surprised look at him.

"What?" Jack smiled. "You think I play golf all day?"

She actually blushed, the soft pink filling her cheeks making him want to touch her. Find out if her skin was as satiny as it looked. He'd had a stingy sample in his office. It had only made him want more.

"Okay, you two. Go on," Evelyn said, and put a warning finger up to Norm when he started to object. "You be quiet. We see Jack all the time. I doubt he wants to waste the night sharing Carly with us old coots."

"I swear to God, Evelyn, you're worse than my wife and I didn't think that was possible." Norm eyed his plate of shrimp as though he'd forgotten about it, and sat down.

"Well, I've had to put up with you longer," Evelyn muttered, then watched with an air of disdain as he tucked his linen napkin under his bearded chin. "Nice meeting you, Carly. I hope we see more of you."

"I don't know," she said with a mischievous smile aimed at Jack. "I'm curious about the bachelor who came in first."

Several moments of shocked silence were punctuated by a chorus of laughter.

"Come on." Shaking his head, Jack took her hand and she let him tug her away from the table.

Figured he'd had to run into Norm right off the bat. Though few employees treated Jack any differently. Except for the damn bear hugs. Man, was he ever going to get it through Norm's thick skull that picking him up hadn't been funny for over twenty years?

That was the thing, these people weren't just employees, they were like a second family to Jack. He'd known half of them his whole life. Nobody ever quit. When they hired someone new it was either to replace a retiree or to fill newly created positions as the company had grown. Carly didn't understand. She probably thought they were all drunk or nuts. Well, some of that was true, too.

Lucky for him the extravagant buffet was the main attraction. For the next hour he shook hands here and there, asked about holiday plans or about wives or husbands who hadn't been able to make it to the party.

Carly stayed by his side the whole time, probably hoping to get a lead on his father. Jack hadn't lied. He didn't know where his old man was hiding. Though Jack hadn't been kidding about the new receptionist. He'd bet his new BMW convertible she had something to do with his dad's absence.

Since that sort of thing didn't seem to bother his mother, Jack shrugged it off. His father was discreet, and she was busy with her pet charities and shopping trips abroad. For all Jack knew, she could have something going on the side, herself.

Okay, that idea creeped him out big-time. Yeah, double standard and all that, and it wasn't as though they had a warm, fuzzy relationship, but shit...

His mom?

A shudder slithered through him.

He snagged a passing waiter and lifted two flutes of champagne off the tray. His parents had always had a weird marriage. If they could call it that. Sleeping in separate bedrooms. Making appointments with each other. He was an only child. They should've split up long ago.

But then, divorces were costly. A guy he knew from college, only thirty-two, Jack's age, had left his wife halfway into their five-year relationship but was staying out of court to protect his assets.

Carly had been right earlier. Everything was about money.

lately and Jack was sick of it. But how sick? How much was he willing to give up to do the right thing? To do what his grandfather and great-grandfather would've expected of him?

"I hope one of those is for me."

He blinked at Carly, then looked at the champagne. "Yes, of course."

She accepted the flute with a small smile, her eyes still clear and focused. He wondered if she knew he was on to her. She'd been sneaking sips from his glass, trying to keep him from getting hammered.

"Hey, you've been great, by the way. I couldn't have asked for a better girlfriend."

"No one believes it," she said, turning away to track a passing tray of stuffed mushrooms.

"Believes what?"

"You should be introducing me as a friend." She looked hungry. And maybe a bit tipsy when she swung her gaze back to him. "Girlfriend? Too extreme. I'm not your type."

"Which is?"

"Oh, I don't know…" She straightened and glanced around. "Someone more sophisticated and glamorous."

"Don't bother looking for her in this crowd." He realized that had come out wrong when Carly stared at him as if he was the biggest snob on earth.

That was, until she was distracted by another tray of hors d'oeuvres.

He stopped the waiter. Pretty obvious the caviar hadn't been a hit. "Carly, you should eat something."

She frowned at the offering. "Is that what I think it is?"

"It's caviar. The same very good caviar you dismissed earlier."

"If it's so good, then why is there so much left?"

The older, very dignified looking waiter hid a smile.

Jack hadn't expected many of the employees to like it but he knew they'd get a kick out of bragging they'd had some.

"Try it," he said, scooping up a little for her. "You might be surprised."

After a brief hesitation, she gamely nibbled at the edge of the cracker. Two rapid blinks, followed by a quick gulp of champagne. "Good," she said, clearly lying through her teeth.

"Here you go." Keeping a straight face, he passed her a cocktail napkin in case she wanted to ditch the rest. "Care for more?"

"No, thanks, you go right ahead."

"Not me. I hate the stuff."

Carly gave him a long look, then laughed.

Jack eyed the mound of caviar, then the waiter's nametag. "Tell you what, Omar, you and the rest of the waitstaff help yourselves in the back."

"Thank you, sir," he said, the reverence in his tone indicating that Omar was a man who appreciated the finer things in life.

"Let's go eat," Jack said, slipping an arm around Carly. "That prime rib looks damn good."

She leaned against his chest without a sign of discomfort and he wondered if her ease was a result of the champagne or something more personal. Wishful thinking on his part that it could be anything but alcohol, but he wasn't about to look a gift horse in the mouth. Carly snuggled closer and he tightened his arm around her. She smelled good. Fresh and kind of minty. And she felt even better, the warmth of her skin coming through the silk blouse. Her body was firm, toned without being too muscled, just the way he liked a woman to feel. Slowly turning his head, he lightly kissed her hair.

"Watch it, Carrington. I felt that," she muttered, her sleepy voice reducing the warning to a faint slur.

Yep. The champagne and the time difference were getting to her. Some food would help. He took the glass out of her hand and set it on an empty table.

"Hey, I'm not done with that." Pulling away, she watched him drain his own flute before setting it aside. "Dammit."

With a smile, Jack took her shoulders and turned her toward the buffet. "First dinner, then coffee."

"This isn't a social—"

"Carly." He hoped she wasn't so tipsy she'd say something stupid.

She turned around to face him and they locked gazes. He wasn't sure what that gleam in her eye was about but he didn't like it. The thing was, she owed him nothing, certainly not discretion, considering he'd put her in a tight spot.

For several long moments they just stared at each other.

"You've gotta do better than that, Jacko." Norm stood near the hall to the men's restroom adjusting a fake white beard that was part of his Santa costume. "Or you're going to be single again real fast."

Jack couldn't figure out what the guy was talking about, until he looked up to see what Norm was pointing at.

Mistletoe. Tied to a beam directly above them.

Carly tilted her head back and blinked at the fresh sprigs.

"What do you say?" Jack stroked her silky cheek and brought her gaze back to his. "Willing to take one for the team?"

"We're not a team," she murmured, and leaned into him.

6

JACK'S HANDS TIGHTENED on her arms. His pupils were huge, darkening his eyes. It would be easy to tell him no. He wouldn't push. But the urge to kiss him was stronger than her good sense. She didn't care that everyone was watching. Didn't care that she was hiding behind the charade as an excuse.

Placing her palms on his chest was all it took. He put his arms around her and pulled her against his body. It wasn't smart. Pressing against each other like they were, sharing each other's heat, ratcheted up the tension. A chaste kiss was all they should dare. She lifted her mouth to him. Disappointment flooded her when his lips barely touched hers.

Before she could draw back he angled his head to deepen the kiss. His hand pressed into the small of her back at the same moment she felt his tongue dampen her lips. Panic flared inside her. This was only supposed to be for show.

He lifted his head and captured her gaze. "Kiss me back," he said in a low husky murmur, and resettled his mouth on hers.

Was he crazy? She could feel him getting hard. They had an audience. Half the people in the room were watching. Maybe the whole lot of them.

Oh, God. Now they were applauding.

She jerked back, squirmed as desire fought propriety.

"Yes. Okay. Give me a minute." He loosened his arms but clearly he wasn't about to let her go. "All right, everyone, get back to your boozing and debauchery. You're embarrassing Carly," he said without taking his gaze off her face.

"*You're* embarrassing me," she muttered, the floor shifting under her feet. Between the alcohol and those damn sexy eyes of his, she wasn't feeling very steady.

"Debauchery? What the hell does that mean?"

Carly recognized Norm's booming voice and she broke eye contact to glance at him. He was frowning and scratching under his fake beard.

A few people were still staring at her and Jack. The rest were distracted by the festive desserts being carried to the buffet table. She lowered her hands from his chest, aware that his erection hadn't completely gone down.

"Thanks for playing along. Tell Brent I appreciate the loan."

"Who?" She blinked. Oh, that Brent. The one who was supposed to be her boyfriend. Damn Jack and his amused expression. "Why is Norm wearing a Santa suit? There aren't any kids here," she said, glancing around.

"Tradition. Later he'll take presents the employees have donated to a children's hospital. He's been doing it for over twenty years." His shoulders sagged as he slowly surveyed the room with a sadness that tugged at her heart.

Not her problem, she reminded herself. He and his father agreed to sell their company. No one had put a gun to their heads.

That was the simple truth. Though not as comforting as it should be.

A loud screech hurt her ears and momentarily drowned out the music being played by the DJ. Like everyone else Carly turned to the source. Four stocky men were moving tables and putting them against the wall.

"How about we get some food and take it to my office?" Jack glanced at the area being cleared. "People are going to start dancing any minute."

"Really?" She grinned. "I bet you've got a full dance card."

He sighed. "I'm fixing a plate and taking it upstairs. Feel free to join me."

Carly followed him to the table, amused that he hadn't

bothered to look back. He wouldn't trust her alone down here for a minute.

Evelyn was choosing from a platter of petit fours. She looked up and smiled. "You two are just so cute together," she said. "I'm so happy for Jack."

Uncomfortable, Carly forced herself to smile, and slid a look at him. He was waiting for a slice of prime rib at the other end. He might've heard but she couldn't tell.

The older woman leaned closer to Carly. "He didn't like that eligible bachelor foolishness. The day after the magazine came out he took off for Barbados or Bermuda…one of those places."

Ah, that's why the winter tan.

"I've known that boy since he was five. Splashing his picture all over a magazine? What was Bernard thinking? He's in charge of Marketing." She dismissively waved a hand. "Jack's always been a hard worker. Did you know he got top honors from Yale Law?"

Carly jerked her gaze to Jack, who was still loading his plate. Ryan had gone to Yale. They were about the same age. Had they known each other in school? Was she missing something here?

"You didn't know," Evelyn said with a pleased smile. "I'm not surprised. He's not one for tooting his own horn. I do wish his grandfather was still around. Eldon would be so proud of him."

Carly's gaze automatically went to Jack. No, he couldn't hear over the music. "Have you seen Mr. Carrington tonight? Jack's father?"

"No, as a matter of fact, I haven't…" Evelyn glanced over her shoulder. "Jackson never spends much time at company gatherings. He'll pop in, make a toast, shake a few hands. He's nothing like his father or Jack. But his assistant is right over there." Evelyn's little sniff indicated exactly what she though of the thirtysomething blonde in the tight red dress. "You can bet Lila knows exactly where he is and what he's doing."

Evidently Evelyn didn't know about the new receptionist, Carly thought, and watched Lila scan the room, looking pissed. Nope, his assistant couldn't find him either. And Carly would bet Lila had a good idea she had some competition.

Jack joined them, dinner in one hand and a glass of wine in the other. "Where's your plate?"

"Looks as if you have enough for both of us."

"I'm not sharing." He leaned against Carly. "Unless there's a kiss in it for me."

Evelyn beamed at them. "So cute," she muttered and wandered over to the other desserts.

Carly rolled her eyes at him. And ignored her speeding pulse just thinking there might be another kiss.

"I'm serious," he said. "You should grab something—"

"Jacko, wait—" It was Norm hurrying toward them. He signaled to the DJ, and the music stopped.

Jack glanced at her as if whatever was about to happen was somehow her fault.

"Somebody get me a glass of champagne," Norm barked over his shoulder as he parked himself in front of them. "And one for Carly."

She started to object but felt a sudden wave of tension coming from Jack.

"What are you doing, Norm?" he asked, his voice tight, his face darkening.

Someone handed a flute to Norm, then put one in Carly's hand. The grim expression on Jack's face made her feel like a traitor just for accepting the champagne.

He swore under his breath. "Let's go."

"Now, hold on. This will only take a minute." Norm blocked their way. "I want to do this before your old man shows up."

"I know what you're doing, and while I appreciate the sentiment…but don't."

"Everybody, listen up," Norm bellowed and the murmurs quieted. Over a hundred people were staring at the big man and Jack. "This has been some party, hasn't it?"

Applause, whistles, nods all around.

"And we all know who we have to thank for it, don't we?" The man put his arm around Jack's shoulders.

"Goddamn it, Norm," he mumbled low and frustrated.

"Hell, I'm not just talking about him going all out with the crab, prime rib and things I can't pronounce," Norm continued, getting a few chuckles and ignoring Jack's obvious unease. "We couldn't ask for a better boss. He looks out for the little guys. I'm a shop steward and I probably shouldn't be saying this—"

"Then don't," Jack muttered.

Norm grinned and squeezed his shoulder. "I know what I'm talking about when I tell you this man never cuts corners when it comes to safety and he's always fought to make sure we all made a living wage. Jack's a chip off the old block. I'm referring to his grandfather, may God rest Eldon's soul. And his great-granddad from what I've heard. So how about we raise a glass to our boss…"

The crowd's enthusiastic response drowned out anything else Norm had to say. Carly perfunctorily lifted her flute along with everyone else but she was preoccupied with the emotion Jack was trying to hide. He kept shaking his head, forcing brief smiles, avoiding eye contact. Including hers.

It didn't matter. She could still see the pain in his face. The devastation. The guilt that was eating at him. She couldn't begin to imagine how horrible he felt standing in front of all these people. She didn't want to feel sorry for him. This was partly his doing. He'd had plenty of time to bow out before zero hour. If he had, she'd be on a bus home right now. But then, she'd never have seen Jack again.

"Hey," she said loud enough for Norm to hear. "Can we go eat before the food gets cold?"

Jack met her eyes, surprise and gratitude easing away the pain. Neither of them could seem to look away.

"Speech!" a man at the back shouted.

"Speech!" someone in front echoed, before the word became a roaring anthem.

Norm held up a hand. "Everybody shut up so he can talk."

Jack gave her a wry smile before turning to the crowd. "Thank you," he said. "I wish I'd fed you hot dogs."

Everyone laughed.

He said something privately to Norm, then Jack motioned to the stairs. Carly led the way. The music resumed, and thankfully no one tried to stop them. It wasn't until they were alone in his office that she remembered she was supposed to be hunting down his father.

She watched Jack set the plate of food and the drink he hadn't touched on his desk. "I'm sorry," she said. "I know that was hard."

"No one to blame but myself." He pulled out his desk chair. "Here. Go ahead and eat. If it's too cold we have a microwave up here." He frowned. "Somewhere."

She was still annoyed with him. He'd been a jackass and might cost her Christmas at home. At the same time she felt badly for him. God knew she had her share of regrets. Had done things she'd wished she could take back.

"Eat," he said. "You need something to soak up that booze you've been mainlining."

"Me?"

"I don't want to find you dancing naked on the buffet table."

She choked out a laugh. "I'm not that tipsy."

"Now, if you wanted to use my desk for a private show I wouldn't object."

"How generous. I'll be sure to file that one away."

With a wicked smile he came around his desk and took

her hand. He only drew her to his chair, but still… Way to give her a cardio workout. Jeez.

"This is your plate," she said, then scooped up a stuffed cherry tomato when her stomach growled.

"We'll share it. How's that?"

Way too intimate, but she was starving.

And she had questions. One in particular, and she needed him relaxed. With his guard down and concentrating on the food, she might get a truthful answer.

Jack dragged a club chair closer to the desk. He sat down opposite her and gave her a lazy smile, the kind that had probably snagged him the title of Chicago's second most eligible bachelor.

Carly smiled back, letting the moment breathe before she pounced. "How do you know Ryan Dunn?" she asked, watching for Jack to flinch.

7

HE DIDN'T EVEN BLINK. Instead he gave her a funny look. "See what I mean about the booze? Didn't he send you?"

"I meant before this. Did you know him?"

"Not really. We both went to Yale. I was a year behind and we never interacted. It's clear he doesn't remember me."

"Yet you remember him."

"He was kind of a—" Jack gave in to a faint smile. "Memorable. Look in that top right drawer, would you? I might have an extra fork in there."

"Ryan has his good points." She found wrapped plastic utensils and a silver fork mixed in with the paper clips. Ewww. She gave him the flatware from downstairs and kept the plastic for herself. "Like sending me here. He was doing me a favor."

Jack leaned back and gave her a slow, considering look. "Get out—" His eyes narrowed. "You asked to come?"

"Yep. Just to see you." She held in a laugh for as long as she could. Then lost it the second she saw that he realized she was teasing.

His shock faded to annoyance. "All right," he muttered, shaking his head.

"This case we have, it's a mess, and now we're looking for something the prosecutor buried. We go back to court right after Christmas so it's been crazy. I'm supposed to be on vacation. But I've been working nonstop along with the other paralegals. Ryan told everyone to cancel their holiday plans until we find it."

"So sending you here gave him a reason to pull you off the case and still make it home."

"Exactly."

"I see. So you should be thanking me."

"I'll thank you to hand me a signed contract."

"You're supposed to be on vacation so Ryan's not really doing you a solid."

Of course Jack had a point. She'd thought the same thing. Not that she'd admit it. "Have you ever worked in a law office?"

"Does the ACLU count?"

That stopped her for a moment. "Well, you must've worked long hours sometimes."

"Many times." He wiped his fork off with the linen napkin. "Now at least I understand why you're cranky."

"I don't give a crap about working long hours. I do it all the time between my job and law school." She paused, pleased to see she'd surprised him again. "I'm not cranky. I'm disappointed that you've reneged on the deal."

He didn't even blink. "Law school, huh? Night classes?"

She nodded. "Now, can we get back to business?"

"You hoping to work for Abbott and Flynn?"

"Yes." She hated the doubt she saw in his eyes. Did he think she didn't have the right stuff for a firm like Abbott and Flynn? Or was he being a snob about night school? Screw him. Not everyone could afford Yale. She was a great paralegal and she'd be a great attorney.

"How much longer do you have?"

"I'm done in six months."

"That's tough. Working days, school at night. Good for you." He cut off a bite of meat and chewed thoughtfully. "Abbott and Flynn doesn't deserve you. They promise you anything yet?"

"I haven't really said much. Except to Ryan." She was still recovering from his reaction. Abbott and Flynn didn't deserve her? "Quit trying to butter me up. I want that contract in my hands before midnight. Signed. Understood?"

"Did Ryan say he'd help you with the partners when the time came?"

"That's none of your business."

"You're right. It's not." Jack smiled. "Did he?" He waited for her to answer, and when she stayed silent, he said, "Don't trust him, Carly. The guy's a weasel."

"I thought you didn't know Ryan."

"You forget, I was in negotiations with him for months. I don't like the way he does business. Abbott, either. Only difference with him is the pearly whites are showing while he goes for the jugular."

She felt her defenses spring up. "I've heard our criminal and divorce teams can be somewhat ruthless but—"

"Somewhat?"

"But," she repeated, annoyed with his condescending tone. "Their reputations are sterling. They operate within the law."

"Look, I'm not trying to cast aspersions on your firm."

"Could've fooled me."

"This is personal, between you and me," he said, shaking his head. "I'm just asking you to be careful. Of Ryan. He can lie right to your face and you won't see it coming."

"No? And what? You know this because we've become so well acquainted in the last…" She glanced at her watch. Oh, God. "Four hours?"

"Well, I can already tell you're a terrible liar."

"Really?" She lifted her chin, pretending he'd just struck out. Unfortunately, he was right. "How would you know?"

Jack looked at her with that damnable expression of amusement he had down to a science. "Who's Brent?" he asked. "Your brother?"

"No. I told you—" She could feel her face heating. "Would I lie about someone being deployed? You think I could be that despicable?"

"Poor guy probably is being deployed. I'm not questioning that. Who is he?"

"Not my brother."

Jack grinned. "A cousin?"

"Shut up." She speared another cherry tomato with her

plastic fork and stuffed it into her mouth to give herself a chance to think. After chewing it to death and swallowing, she said, "I may have stretched the truth a little."

"There you go. Already on your way to being a good lawyer."

She sighed. "Brent used to be my boyfriend, okay? In high school."

"Ah. You gave him the old heave-ho and now you're feeling guilty because he's being shipped off."

"Wrong. *He* dumped *me*."

Jack leaned back with a frown. "Fool." He looked adorably indignant. Even if he was just kidding around.

"I really do want to spend Christmas with my folks. It's been three years since I've had the time and money to get there. And yes, I wanted to see Brent. I knew he'd be in town on Christmas Eve. The neighborhood is giving him a send-off party tomorrow night."

"Very admirable that you want to see him."

"Nothing admirable about it. He dumped me to marry Loretta Parsons. She was the hottest girl in school, whose father also happened to own the largest factory in town. Most of the other fathers worked there, including mine." She shrugged. "I heard Loretta isn't looking so hot these days and her father went bankrupt and…"

"You wanted to show old Brent what he missed out on." Jack let out a laugh. "Good for you."

"Don't laugh at that. It isn't funny. I'm a pathetic human being. That's why I'm stranded here. It's karma."

"You aren't stranded." Laughter still gleamed in his eyes. "Oh, yeah, and you're not pathetic either."

Rubbing her left temple, she tamped down a smile. "Really I just wanted Brent to see that I'm making something of myself. It would've been sweeter if I was already out of school but having only six months to go is pretty awesome. For my neighborhood, anyway. It's a steel town. Very blue-collar. Expectations aren't high."

"The guy sounds like an opportunist. Better that you got rid of him, right?"

"Oh, yeah, I wasn't that crazy about him, anyway. It's just stupid pride." She met Jack's watchful eyes. What the hell was she doing telling him all this? She heard a muffled buzzing noise and straightened. "Is that your phone? Maybe it's your father."

"That's not me." He glanced at her things on the couch. "You sure that's not you?"

"Oh, jeez." She got to her feet and hurried over. Her phone was buried under her bag and coat, and the generic ringtone meant it could finally be Mavis. It sure wasn't Ryan, the jerk.

Carly stared at the text. According to Mavis, Ryan had left the office hours ago to attend a friend's party.

Anger flared inside her. Irrational, maybe. It wasn't as if his waiting around the office would help her any. But he should've answered her texts. If Jack refused to sign the contract, there was nothing she could do. She had no reason to stay in Chicago. But Ryan had to give her the green light so she could catch a flight home.

The thought made her uneasy.

Was Ryan deliberately avoiding her? Was he hoping he could somehow pin this mess on her?

Or was she being paranoid because of Jack's warning?

"Are you okay?"

She looked over at Jack. "Yeah. Fine." She wondered if she should push him for more information on Ryan. She could tell he was holding back. And while she admired his restraint, she didn't want to be flying without a compass.

"You don't look fine."

She turned away from his speculative gaze. "It's snowing. Kind of hard. Should I be worried about the airport closing?"

Jack snorted. "We're tough here in Chicago. Not like you wussy New Yorkers."

Carly laughed. "Wussy? I don't think that's a common perception of us."

"You're not a true New Yorker. You're a transplant. And too nice."

"Um, not really."

Carly watched Jack's mouth curve into a smile as he pushed to his feet. The kind of roguish smile that made her hold her breath and take two steps back.

SECONDS BEFORE JACK was about to kiss her, her phone startled them. Cursing his luck, he moved to the window to watch the snow come down as she answered the call.

"Mom? It's late. Anything wrong?" Apparently she didn't care that he could hear her because she stayed put. "No, I'm in Chicago. It's snowing here, too, but not that much." She laughed softly. "No, I flew. The trip was unexpected. It's business." Carly sighed. "Of course it's safe, Mom. Planes fly in snow all the time."

Jack wanted to look at her. He'd bet anything she was smiling while she reassured her mother. But he stayed focused on the falling snow against the black sky and the distant downtown lights. As a kid he'd loved sneaking up to the rooftop to watch the snow fall. Back then he could see more of the skyline.

"I hope first thing in the morning," she said, something Jack absorbed with mixed feelings.

He had no right to want her to stay longer. Hell, it was the holidays and she had a life. She had a family who wanted her with them.

"Don't worry. I'll still make it. And yes, I'll be careful. Get some sleep." Carly paused, and laughed. "I figured as much. Tell Dad to have a hot toddy. Oh, what the heck—you, too, it's almost Christmas." She laughed again at something her mom said. "I love you, too. Yes, I promise. But I really have to go now."

She moved closer, but it was hard to look at her. Overhearing her conversation made him feel like shit. Even though this whole thing was on Ryan. No, that wasn't fair. Jack was equally to blame.

"My mom's never flown before so she gets nervous. My dad, too." She almost sounded apologetic. "As soon as he found out I was in Chicago he switched to the weather channel."

"That's nice."

"I know," she said, sighing and looking up at the sky. "I say I'm from Pittsburgh but actually I grew up in a small town outside the city. So did my parents, except they rarely leave the neighborhood."

"I wasn't being snide. I think it's nice that they worry about you."

"Well, of course they would. They're my parents."

Jack started to comment, but then why subject her to his cynicism? All parents weren't created equal. Some cared more about their standing spa appointments.

"What?"

"Nothing." His silence had no effect on her. She stared unabashedly at him, waiting, and he shrugged. "Your parents sound like good salt-of-the-earth people. I'm glad for you."

She laid a hand on his arm, surprising him. He met her eyes and she gave him a smile. A very sweet smile that he didn't deserve. A smile that made him feel worse than the guilt had a few minutes ago.

Before she could say something that would make him feel like an even bigger jerk, he said, "I can't do it, Carly. I can't sign the contract."

"I know." Her smile faded some but didn't disappear.

"I'm sorry. I really am. I hate that you're involved."

"For what it's worth, I totally understand, and I think you're doing the right thing."

"I'm not being noble. I brought this on myself and everyone else. All because I'm a damn coward." Exhaling, he stared out at the snow. "Anyway, your obligation is officially over. Call the airlines, find a flight, go be with your family."

"Hush," she whispered, and kissed him.

8

THEIR LIPS TOUCHED. Carly had meant to give him a light kiss. Just enough contact to pull him back from the dark mood enveloping him. But her heart had started racing and maybe she was a little tipsy because standing on her tiptoes almost made her lose her balance.

Jack's arms came around her. She hesitated, only for a second or two, then slid her hands up his chest to the back of his neck. His lips were firm and sure moving over hers, his arms tightening until she was flush against him. His heart beat as fiercely as her own.

She leaned into him, soaking in the solid warmth of his body and fighting off a shiver when his hand stroked the curve of her lower back. His tongue followed the edge of her bottom lip then slid inside her mouth. He tasted like champagne and something sweet, something that could get her into a lot of trouble.

Her breasts had started to ache. She told herself to pull back. This kiss was going further than she'd intended. It was unprofessional. Crazy. Not like her at all. So he'd finally admitted he wasn't signing the contract. That wasn't her cue to forget she was still representing Abbott and Flynn. Things wouldn't end here just because he'd changed his mind. Too much money was at stake. A lawsuit was likely.

And Jack could use her behavior against her and the firm if he chose.

The sudden thought had her jerking back.

He blinked, clearly startled. His gaze went to the phone still in her hand. "What's wrong?"

"I'm sorry," she said, slipping free of him and walking toward the desk. "We're not pretending for the employees anymore. My obligation may be over for now, but it was still unprofessional, and I hope we can move past this without it becoming an issue—" She swallowed around a lump of humiliation and met his gaze. "Or becoming public knowledge."

Anger flared in his eyes. She hadn't seen him mad before and it was a bit unsettling. She tried to swallow again but couldn't.

Jack shoved a hand through his hair, the anger leaving his face. "You have nothing to worry about from me. Blackmail and coercion…" He shook his head. "I'm not that much of a bastard. Though working with Dunn I understand why you might be paranoid."

"That's the second time you've implied Ryan's underhanded. I'm not saying you're lying or wrong, I just don't get where this attitude is coming from."

He stared at her for a long prickly moment. "I have no illusions about the consequences I'll be facing by quashing the deal. Legally, financially, it's going to cost me a fair chunk…" His mouth curved in a faint smile. "I might need a good lawyer. When did you say you'll be taking the bar?"

Carly still thought he was being noble, but also foolish. She sighed. "How can you joke about this?"

He took her hand. "Only one thing worries me, Carly. I'm afraid Ryan will try to hang you out to dry on this. And while I'm certain I can run interference, I can't promise you won't suffer some backlash."

"Quit being so damn cryptic."

"I'm saying that you probably won't lose your job, but Abbott and Flynn will never hire you as an attorney."

"Not that I'm going to let that remark go, but what's the deal with you and Ryan? Why are you so confident that you can make him back down?"

He let go of her hand and started to walk away, but she caught his arm.

"I'm a big girl, Jack. You can tell me."

He studied her for a moment, clearly hesitant. "Ryan is using you. He figured you had the best chance of convincing me to sign."

"Me? That doesn't make sense. Before tonight, we barely spoke—" She remembered Ryan's comment about Jack's attraction to her.

With a wry smile, he said, "True, but I'd noticed you right away. Ryan picked up on it." He cleared his throat. "We were close to making a deal but I had a problem with some ambiguous language. You'd been coming in and out of the meeting supplying Ryan with documents. We were frustrated and he suggested we finish in the morning." He paused, clearly taking no pleasure in what he was about to tell her. "On your way out of the conference room, he nodded at you and said if I was interested, he could make it happen."

Carly blinked. She couldn't move or speak. No, Jack must've misunderstood. Ryan wouldn't have offered her up as if she was nothing more than a bargaining chip. He respected her. "I'm sure he didn't mean—"

The pained expression on Jack's face made her stop. He was very certain of Ryan's meaning. And this hadn't been easy for him. He'd wanted to spare her, but he hadn't wanted her to be caught unaware either.

"I'm sorry, Carly. I'm very sorry."

She stayed outwardly calm. Inside she was shaking so badly she wasn't sure she should trust her voice. "What did you say to him?"

"I almost punched the bastard. But then, explaining myself would've made everything worse. So, I just walked away. It was one of the hardest and most adult decisions I've ever made."

Carly smiled but she was still jittery. Her stomach was a giant knot and her breathing was off.

"Look, if he plays dirty with you, a private reminder should be enough to get him to back off. He doesn't need the senior partners knowing about his dumbass move or worrying about a sexual harassment lawsuit. But if it makes you uncomfortable, I won't say another word about the incident."

"Frankly, I think I'm in shock. I'm not sure how I'm going to handle it." Hugging herself, she turned to the window. She and Ryan had had some really fun times. How could he? "I won't make it easy for him to fire me or even put a reprimand in my file. I'm not leaving here until he gives me the go-ahead. He's banking on me giving up. I bet that's why he's ignoring my texts."

"You can leave. How will he know?"

"The company bought my ticket. I can't afford to buy another one."

"I'll cover it."

"No," she said sharply, turning to him. "Sorry, didn't mean to bite your head off."

Jack smiled. He'd moved closer, right behind her. He circled his arms around her and pulled her against his chest. "Part of this mess is your fault."

"How?" She tried to look at him but he pressed a kiss to the side of her neck, and she decided they could talk just as easily with her staying snug in his arms.

"At one point during negotiations you'd come into the conference room and stood to the side waiting to slip Ryan a note. We were discussing which employees were needed to make the transition smoothly. It was like a giant chess game. In the end a few managers would still have their jobs, assuming they were willing to relocate to New Jersey. No one cared about the employees who were being cut loose. It was all about the bottom line. Do you remember?"

She nodded. Oh, she remembered. Despite working for attorneys for years and going to law school herself, the casual disregard for people who'd worked so hard for so long had made her doubt herself. Made her wonder if she was following the right career path.

"I was right in the middle of the whole thing, getting off on the negotiating, showing off my skills. And then I saw your face. You looked so damned sad. I was ashamed. I walked out of there feeling like I'd just made a deal with the devil."

"Funny, I remember you fighting for the employees. You were pushing for huge severance packages. Everyone else thought you were crazy."

"Hey, at least I had some conscience." He released her and rubbed his eyes. "People working here aren't doing it for the money. They're loyal and take pride in their work. They go to each other's kids' weddings and grandchildren's baptisms. Everyone's family."

"Including you."

"Yeah, I'm a real prince."

"Stop beating up on yourself. You weren't the only one who wanted to sell." She saw her words made no impact. He stared gloomily out the window. "Okay, you want to know the truth? Yes, I was sad for the people being displaced. For all of ten seconds. Then it was all about me. I was terrified that I'd made the wrong choice, that I didn't have the backbone to be a good attorney."

"Ah, right, you have compassion." He looked at her with a faint smile. "What a disgusting trait."

"I'm serious. It was a horrible feeling. I'd spent so much money, time and effort on law school. My father loves telling everyone his daughter is a lawyer." She sighed. "He can't seem to comprehend being a paralegal isn't the same thing."

"There are all kinds of law. You'll find the right fit."

She nodded. "I thought about environmental law, but then I probably wouldn't be working for Abbott and Flynn."

"Why not? Environmental law is cropping up in more and more companies. The world is changing, and they know they have to keep up. I'll bet if they don't have a place for you now, they will soon." Jack reclaimed her hand. "The question is… would you be happy working for them?"

Carly shrugged. "I have a proven track record with them. And the firm is highly regarded and pays well…"

"Duly noted, now answer the question." He held her gaze.

"We're not supposed to be talking about me," she muttered.

"And here I thought you were trying to make me feel better."

"Nope. Just clearing my conscience." She ignored his skeptical smile. "So why did you stay in negotiations? Why didn't you walk away then? Now it's going to cost you."

"I admitted I was a jerk. I didn't say I was stupid," he said with a wry smile. "Backing out won't cost me as much as you might think. I inserted an escape clause. We'll forfeit earnest money, which is a chunk, and I'll have to pay Luxury Lighting's legal fees. Naturally, it'll come out of my own pocket."

"Ryan went for the clause?"

"He missed it at first. But then Dad was eager to sell and Ryan probably figured it was better to push forward than hold things up and risk the partners finding out." He turned back to the window. "The old man's going to be pissed. But I can stay and run the company. As long as we're profitable and he doesn't have to worry about the details, he'll get over it."

"You can stay?" She frowned. "What does that mean?"

"I miss practicing law," he said with a shrug. "I'd never intended to stay with the company full-time. But the longer I was here the harder it was to walk away. When my dad said he'd been approached by Luxury, I figured it was my chance to go do what I should've had the guts to do without screwing everyone over."

Carly slid her arms around his neck. He seemed surprised, and then he smiled and put his hands on her waist. "In the end, you're doing what's right," she said. "Regardless of the potential fallout. That sounds gutsy to me."

"Be sure and mention that to my father, would you?"

"Poor Jack." She massaged the back of his neck. "Will you be grounded over this?"

"I might. But you could keep me company." He pulled her closer, forcing her to tilt her head back so she could look at him. "Did you know I live ten minutes from here?"

"No." She tamped down a smile. "No, I didn't. How is that significant?"

"It's not." He lightly bit her earlobe. "I'll strip you naked right here."

Carly laughed. "Are you propositioning me, Mr. Carrington?" She felt a tug on her blouse, felt it being pulled free of her skirt's waistband. "Wait. Hey, wait," she said, still laughing and fighting his hand at the same time.

"Why?" His lips traced her jaw to that sweet spot below her ear. "Come home with me, Carly," he whispered. "I'll get you on a plane tomorrow, I swear."

She tried to think of something clever to say, maybe tease him a little. She made the mistake of looking into his sexy blue-green eyes, and all she could say was, "Yes."

9

JACK'S MODERN TWO-BEDROOM condo was on the twenty-third floor of a high-rise and overlooked Lake Michigan. Even with all the marble from the foyer to the kitchen counters, the place still managed to look warm and inviting. Though the gleaming hardwood floors had made her hesitate. She would've just died if she'd dinged them with her heels, but Jack assured her that his home was meant to be lived in. That was the only hard-and-fast rule he'd given the decorator.

Carrying her canvas bag, he led her down a short hall, past the guest room and second bathroom. Upon entering his bedroom she gasped. He gave her a sharp inquiring look and she laughed self-consciously.

"This is huge. It's bigger than my whole apartment," she said, eyeing the art deco–inspired sitting area near the window. "Oh, and you have a fireplace in here, too." She sighed. "All I have is a roommate."

"That's New York for you."

"I bet Chicago prices aren't far behind. Especially this Lake Shore Drive stretch." She stared out the window into the darkness. A light flickered and bobbed. "Wait," she said as he started to draw the drapes. "Is that Lake Michigan? You have the same view of the water from here as the living room. Wow."

"The view is much better from here." The husky dip in his voice got her attention. He was looking straight at her.

"That's some line," she said with a nervous laugh. "Use it much?"

"Never."

"Oh." Her hands shook slightly. Butterflies were tap-dancing along her nerve endings. Jeez. This wasn't like her.

Somehow he'd moved behind her and when he touched her shoulders, she jumped.

"I'm just taking your coat, Carly."

"Yeah, thanks." She cleared her throat.

Why was she reacting to him like this now? Before he'd been a good-looking rich guy. Someone her coworkers had tripped over themselves to get a look at every time he came to the office. But not her...she'd been cool as a cucumber. She wished she could find some of that cool now.

Her blazer came off along with the heavy wool coat. He tossed them both on the chair near the window, then turned back to her. "You seem preoccupied," he said, searching her face, his eyes dark and questioning. "Have you changed your mind?"

"About being here? No." She put her hands on his chest. "Actually, I was thinking about how you're not just another pretty face."

Jack grinned. "Fair enough. Since I was thinking the same about you earlier."

"Oh, you're a smooth one," she said, laughing.

"Smooth?" He frowned. "I wasn't—"

Raising on tiptoes she silenced him with a kiss. He went for her buttons, and she yanked his shirt free of his slacks. She was tackling his belt buckle when he drew back.

The safety pin had stopped him.

"Wait," she said. "Let me. I don't want to rip the silk."

"Better hurry." He toed off his shoes and sent the belt flying toward the armoire. His shirt disappeared in record time.

Carefully removing the safety pin took some concentration on her part. When she finally looked up he'd already turned down the taupe quilt and was wearing nothing but a pair of navy blue boxer briefs. His smooth tanned chest was muscled just enough to make her breath catch. He truly was beautiful.

She wished she'd made time to work out more...

Jack took the safety pin out of her hand, then finished free ing the rest of the buttons. Slipping the blouse off her shoulders, he bent his head to kiss the skin above the lacy edge of her pink bra. She had a weakness for good lingerie, even if it meant skimping for weeks to afford the hefty price tags. Totally worth it for this moment alone.

With hurried movements he unhooked the bra while she unzipped her skirt. His hands were on her bare breasts before she could slide the skirt past her hips. She shivered when he cupped their weight, then explored her tight nipples with his fingers, rubbing them, teasing them, sending tiny electric jolts to the damp heat between her thighs.

He nipped at her lips, sucking at the lower one, the slight tug amazingly erotic. "Don't stop," he murmured against her mouth.

"What?" she asked, dizzy from his touch.

With a grunt of impatience, he removed his hands from her breasts and finished sliding the skirt down her thighs.

Clutching his shoulders, she kicked off one high heel. The other went flying in the same direction as his belt. Then so did her skirt. She stood in only her skimpy panties and sheer black thigh-highs.

Jack drew back to take a look. With a slow smile, he cupped her cheek with one hand, lightly stroking her skin with his thumb. Before she knew it, his other hand slipped around to her backside and he firmly pulled her against him.

Her nipples pressed into his chest and they both inhaled sharply. He was already hard and ready, just as she was swollen and wet. But he didn't rush her. Only brushed a light, gentle kiss across her mouth. Wanting more, she leaned harder into him and parted her lips. His tongue slid inside, stroking hers, swirling and tasting, until her whole body started to throb.

He eased back, ignoring her protest. "Let's get these off you," he said, and it took her a moment to realize he meant her panties and thigh-highs.

She glanced down and swayed to the side. He steadied her with one hand on her hip, the other clasping her arm. "You okay?"

She nodded. "Too much champagne."

The intense way he studied her face made her silently curse her big mouth. She should've known better than to blame anything on booze. Jack wasn't the type to take advantage of a woman. If he thought she was even the slightest bit impaired he'd do exactly what he was doing right now…backing off.

"It's not the champagne," she said, catching his arm and tugging him back to her. "I just— I can't quite believe I'm here. With you. Like this."

He didn't seem 100 percent convinced. With surprising tenderness, he swept the bangs out of her eyes. "How about we sleep first? Just a short nap."

Waste time sleeping? "Are you out of your mind?"

"Probably," he said with a smile. "You're tired from working long hours and I don't want you to regret anything later. Or worry that you crossed a line."

"I know exactly what I want. To be right here." She pressed herself against him, loving the feel of hard muscle and warm skin underneath her palm.

He kissed her lips, the side of her mouth, her jaw, and skimmed his hand over the curve of her hip before crouching in front of her. "Nice," he said, tracing a finger along the lacy top of her left thigh-high. "I think we'll leave these on."

"Um, really?" They were ultra sheer and ultra expensive.

Jack smiled. "Don't worry. I break 'em, I buy 'em."

Carly laughed. Great. Now he could read her mind. It was easy to be relaxed with him. Maybe too easy, but for tonight she wouldn't think about such things. She wouldn't even worry about her stupid stockings.

His lips followed the trail of his finger and then he kissed the soft skin between her stockings and panties. Balancing herself, she held on to his shoulders and watched him. His lashes seemed especially thick and long from her position above him, and as hot as he looked clean shaven, the faint stubble shadowing his jaw was definitely doing it for her.

He moved to her lower belly, pressing a kiss there, through the damp silk panties.

Unprepared for the intimate gesture, Carly shuddered. Feeling the slide of his finger underneath the elastic, she clutched at his hair, tensing, waiting to see what he'd do next. Without hesitation he stripped her panties down her legs. Carefully he freed one of her ankles before cupping her backside and pulling her against his mouth.

The first long, slow stroke of his tongue had her fisting his hair more tightly. She automatically clenched and tried to squeeze her thighs together but that made him more determined. He used his fingers to spread her, and used his tongue to drive her wild. She bucked against his mouth, triggering a deep low groan that came from his throat and sent warm breath rolling over her sensitive wet flesh.

"Jack…please." She wanted him naked and horizontal, lying beside her on the bed, bare skin to bare skin. What she got was the firm tip of his tongue circling her clit, two long fingers pushing into her and testing the limits of her control.

She didn't want to climax too quickly, yet she didn't want him to stop. She wanted the pressure to continue to build, wanted the delicious warmth enveloping her body to last forever. And most of all, she wanted him inside her. Soon.

Just not yet. Not when he seemed to know just how to touch her, how to do everything exactly how she liked it. His left hand stayed cupped over her bottom, holding her captive against his mouth. His palm was hot and rough, the slightly callused texture unexpected and arousing against her skin.

His tongue and fingers continued to tease and probe and push her to the brink of insanity, demanding her last shred of control…

She convulsed around him and bit down on her lip to keep

from screaming out. Her body quivered as her muscles contracted, and no matter how much she squirmed, he wouldn't let up. He kept pushing her further and further, and when she thought she couldn't take any more, he pushed her all the way to the edge, prolonging her climax until her knees went weak.

Jack slowly raised himself while rubbing his hands up her back and keeping her steady. "Hold on to me," he said, tightening his arms around her.

Before she could make sense of what he'd said, he scooped her up in his arms and carried her the few feet to his king-size bed. He laid her down gently in the middle, and she stretched out on the decadent satiny bronze sheets. Holding her breath, she watched him get completely and gloriously naked. She'd known he would be amazing, but now the word hardly seemed adequate. Jack was *stunning*.

And all hers for the night.

"I should've asked before now…can I get you anything?" he said. "Some water, maybe?"

Carly thought for a moment. Sending him to the kitchen meant she'd get a great backside view. But no, she was too impatient. "No, thanks."

He opened the nightstand drawer and brought out a whole handful of condoms. Oh, she did like a confident man. But then he leaned over and turned off the lamp, plunging the room into darkness. Barely able to see him, she let go a whimper of frustration.

His low husky laugh didn't help. "Hold on a second."

Her eyes hadn't adjusted yet when flames flared in the fireplace. Startled, she turned back to Jack. Flickering firelight lit his face.

"Not wood-burning," he said, dropping a remote control on the nightstand. "But so much easier."

"Not wood-burning?" she repeated, her hand covering her mouth with shock. "But it looks so convincing. How can I ever trust you?" She inched over when he crawled in beside her.

"You shouldn't. I have all sorts of wicked things in mind… Where do you think you're going?"

"I'm giving you room."

He closed his fingers over her hand, holding it captive. "I want you right here."

Moving with spellbinding grace, he covered her body with his, resting his hips against hers and bracing himself on his elbows so that his chest grazed her breasts. His arousal lay hot and heavy on her stomach and his breath was warm on her face as he looked into her eyes.

"You're beautiful, Carly," he whispered, brushing the hair away from her cheek. "Inside and out."

The sincerity on his face stole the air from her lungs and all her words. This was just sex, she reminded herself. Only pillow talk, and she'd be a fool to forget. She lifted her mouth to him, and he kissed her long, deep and perfect.

10

AFTER SEVERAL ENDLESS MOMENTS, they broke the kiss so they could both breathe. Carly's breasts rising and falling against his chest were driving him insane. Jack had wanted to take his time with her, but he wasn't sure he could hold out long enough. Her hips were moving, putting pressure on his cock, and that alone might be the thing to do him in.

She reached around and squeezed his ass. "You take your workouts seriously," she said, and he grinned.

"Nope. I only use the gym during the winter. When the weather is good I run, play pickup basketball and kick ass on the company's softball team." Okay, this was better. Talking was a good distraction. Only she wouldn't stop moving her hips.

He rolled onto his side.

"Hey." She gave him a fierce little frown that was actually kind of cute. "Why did you do that?"

"Because…" He leaned over and kissed her breast. "You were teasing me."

Shuddering, she strained toward him, her nipple a tight bud and damp from his mouth. "It's not teasing if I plan to go through with it."

"Go through with what?" He caught the mischievous gleam in her eye a second before she wrapped her hand around his cock. Something between a grunt and a laugh slipped out of him. "Easy."

"Am I hurting you?" she asked, eyes wide with fake innocence as she started stroking him.

"Carly…" God, he needed to make her stop. But it felt good. So damn good. Giving up, he fell onto his back and closed his eyes. She knew just how much pressure to use, just when to ease up.

It was tempting to let her keep going but this wasn't how he wanted their first time to go. A few moments later he realized he'd started thrusting his hips. On a deep inhale he froze and caught her wrist. His cock pulsed against her warm palm.

"Please, Jack, let me," she whispered, the raspy need in her voice stoking the fire inside him.

He licked her breast, then sucked the nipple into his mouth while he pried her fingers away from his throbbing erection. She whimpered and he sucked harder. She tasted sweet, so tempting, so responsive. He'd be a fool to think he could last much longer. He slid his free hand between her legs, the back of his knuckles skimming the soft silky skin of her inner thighs, and man, how could that in itself be such a major turn-on?

Finding her wet and ready, he easily slid his finger deep inside her. She gasped, her moist breath washing over his ear in a heated rush. He lifted his head, blew lightly on her damp nipple and then kissed her lips before coaxing her mouth open. Their tongues touched and circled each other. He reminded himself he wasn't in a hurry but that did no good when Carly bucked against his finger.

He inserted a second one, curling it slightly and watching her face, hoping he'd hit that perfect spot to give her pleasure. Her breathing came harsh and fast, and she arched off the bed. Her head tilted back, her lips parted, she panted his name. His cock twitched. In a few moments he wouldn't be able to do anything but bury himself inside her slick wet heat.

She twisted her hand, fighting his grip on her wrist until she broke free. "I want you inside me, Jack," she said, her voice whisper soft. "Please. Now. It has to be now."

With a start, he realized she'd already grabbed a packet off the nightstand. While she tore it open, he kissed the side of her neck, but then quickly took the condom from her because he didn't trust his raging body.

"I can do it," she protested, her gaze lowered on his cock.

"No. I can't take the chance."

Her gaze moved up to his face and she blinked.

He sheathed himself as he watched confusion turn to a small smile of satisfaction.

CARLY FELT FIERCE and powerful. It didn't matter that she was a trembling shivery mess. She'd pushed Jack to his limit. This beautiful, intelligent, compassionate man wanted her. He wasn't faking that look of raw need. A need tinged with desperation. The need for her. She'd never experienced anything like it before.

"Carly?" He spread her thighs wider and got between them. "I'm sorry if this first time goes too fast." He leaned down and kissed her mouth. "I'll make it up to you later," he murmured, and pushed deep inside her.

She was breathless for a moment, from the quick unexpected entry, from the moan trapped in her throat. Her desperate inhale came as a surprise. She must have been holding her breath for too long. Now she was gasping as she wrapped her legs around his waist and he pulled them up higher so he could go deeper.

They groaned at the same time.

His jaw clenched, he rocked his hips against her. Slow, measured movements, she could tell, were taking all of his control. He cupped her face with his hand, the slightly rough texture of his palm pressed against her cheek. He leaned down, one strong arm supporting his weight as he kissed her.

"You don't have to go slow," she whispered. "I'm ready."

A low growl escaped him and he began to move again. Faster, deeper, with more intensity. She gave up her tight grip of the sheets to cling to his shoulders.

He groaned, the otherworldly sound coming from the

depths of his throat and his whole body shuddered. She wrapped her arms around him and was startled when the first shock wave swept over her. She could hear the thudding of her heart. Feel the heat rush through her veins. He gathered her in his arms and, with his body, pressed her into the soft mattress, kissing her face and neck while she weathered the storm.

Jack waited until the shuddering stopped and their breathing had slowed, then holding her tight, he rolled onto his back. She ended up on top of him, her breasts pressed against his chest, her arms feeling like rubber. She didn't know how he'd managed it. She was too weak to move a muscle.

"Hi." He untangled the hair from her lashes and smiled.

"Hi, yourself." She let her head drop to his chest. "I can't move."

"You don't have to." He stroked a hand down her back. "Try to sleep."

She rubbed her cheek against his warm skin. She really was groggy. "Maybe a short nap," she said, and tried to move off him. But Jack tightened his arms and kept her right where she was.

CARLY REALIZED SHE'D have to open her eyes eventually. Just not yet. Knowing she was still in Jack's bed was enough for now. His ridiculous high-thread-count sheets had her spoiled for life. She arched her back, stretched out her arms, then her legs. And tried not to wince at the soreness between her thighs. She'd gone too long without, and then made up for it all in one night.

But boy, what a night. There'd been everything but fireworks.

Finally, she forced herself to open her eyes. Mostly because she thought she smelled coffee. She turned her head and saw Jack entering the bedroom carrying a tray. He wore a smile and nothing else.

And already her exhausted body was responding. Good grief.

"We have coffee, water, orange juice and aspirin if you still have a headache." He set the tray down at the foot of the bed, then sat at the edge and kissed her. "How are you feeling?"

"Actually, it's not my head so much that's aching."

He thought for a moment. "Ah. Sorry."

"I'm not complaining," she said. "I've been so busy working lately, you probably saved me from atrophy."

Jack laughed. "No, we wouldn't want that." He caught the hand she'd placed on his chest and lightly kissed her fingertips. "I'll have to be more creative for a while."

A shiver slid through her. From the look in his eyes, he wasn't bluffing. They weren't done. She pulled up the sheet to hide the goose bumps. "Right now, I need coffee. Seriously. Or I will have a headache. I live on caffeine."

"That's not good. We'll have to see what we can do about that." He got up to go to the tray and he was already half-hard. "I brought milk and sugar. I don't have cream."

She was trying to tell him she'd drink it black but the words weren't coming. Between his obvious physical desire for her and his casual use of *we* she was getting a little dizzy.

"You want me to fix it for you or bring you the tray?"

"Just black would be good," she said finally, and looked away. Her gaze landed on the digital clock. She blinked. "It's 2:15. Afternoon or morning?"

She looked to him but she already knew. Sunlight was seeping in from the draped windows.

"Carly, relax."

"I'm so screwed. Why didn't you wake me?"

"I only got up half an hour ago myself. Here, drink."

She waved away the red mug. "I don't have time." She fought her way out of the sheets and swung her feet to the floor.

"You do." He set the mug on the nightstand. "I've checked with the airlines. Come here."

She wasn't sure she liked that he could be this calm. He knew she wanted to go see her family. "I've never slept this late in my entire life," she said as he put his arms around her. It wasn't good news. She could feel it. "Just tell me. Can I get on a flight?"

"Not today, I'm afraid. It's Christmas Eve and lots of people are camping out at the airport hoping for cancellations."

"Oh, God. Did you only check flights to Pittsburgh? Maybe I can fly back to New York and get to Pittsburgh from there."

"I doubt it. Look, I know you want to make it to Brent's party tonight—"

"I don't care about that anymore." She pulled away, shaking her head. "I don't. But my folks—I can't disappoint them."

"You won't." He caught her face between his hands. "You have two choices. I found a flight open tomorrow evening. Or I can drive you."

"To Pittsburgh?" She let out a laugh. "Do you know how far that is?"

"We can get cleaned up and leave in half an hour. Obviously you still wouldn't make the party—"

Carly put a silencing finger on his lips. She could tell he meant it. All she had to do was say the word. She looped her arms around his neck. "What about your Christmas plans? Wouldn't your family miss you?"

He looked at the clock. "My parents are boarding a plane right about now. They're headed to their home in Barbados for a week."

"So your father wouldn't be here when the sale went through…"

"Yep." Jack sighed. "Man, is he in for a surprise."

Carly smiled. Of course Jack wasn't looking forward to that confession but he seemed calm, not resigned either, but relaxed. As if he understood he'd done the right thing and that's what mattered. He'd also taken her need to go home seriously, which she appreciated.

"You could come with me," she said. "Flying or driving, it doesn't matter. My folks are pretty nice people."

He drew back, frowning.

"Or not." She breathed in deeply. "I didn't mean to overstep. I have no assumptions about us. I promise."

Jack pulled her closer. "Maybe you should. Who knows where this could lead?" He looked into her eyes, a tentative smile curving his mouth. "Don't you want to find out?"

Carly had a little trouble finding her voice. That this gorgeous confident man could have the slightest uncertainty that she wanted him for more than a night made her like him twice as much. "Yes," she whispered, then nodded in case it wasn't loud enough.

"I'm thinking a nice long drive will give us plenty of time to discuss our options." He drew her back onto the bed and into his arms. "And in the meantime..."

* * * * *